SIN TAX

A ONE EYED JACK NOVEL

BY

CHRISTOPHER J. LYNCH

SIN TAX

ISBN 0990727319
ISBN-13 978-0-9907273-1-6

Permission to use the name of The Kettle Restaurant in Manhattan Beach granted by The Kettle management.

ACKNOWLEDGMENTS

This book would have not have been possible without the assistance of several people:

Captain Tony Best, Palos Verdes Police Department - for his information regarding vehicular suicides.

Eric Osmond - for his knowledge of everything video editing.

Jeffery M. Teubner of Rotocraft Support Inc. - for his knowledge of helicopter flight and powerplant systems.

Captain Jim Hone, Ret. Santa Monica Fire Department - for his information on first responder protocols.

Kate Stewart at EbookEditingServices.com - for having a keen eye, a ton of patience, and a big eraser.
www.ebookeditingservices.com

Digital Donna - for helping me with yet another awesome cover.
http://digitaldonna.com

Ebook Launch Formatting - for taking my manuscript and making it stand out.
www.ebooklaunch.com

One Eyed Jack's black viper snakeskin eye patch courtesy of Gambles Gifts. www.gamblesgifts.com

Dedication

To my wife Charlotte.

My life, my love.

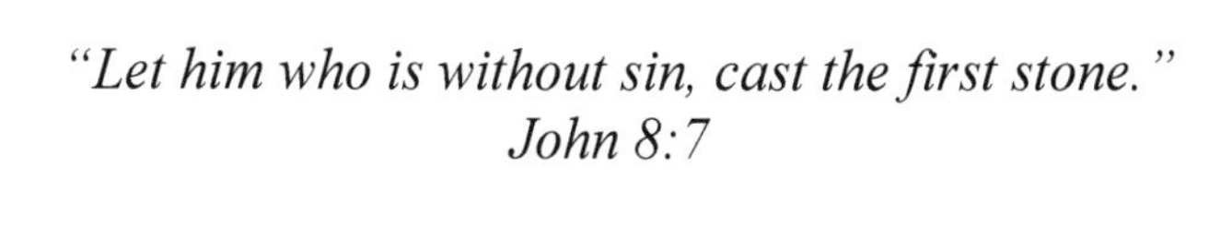

"Let him who is without sin, cast the first stone."
John 8:7

"And those among you who have plenty of sin, watch out for me."
One Eyed Jack 2015

ONE

"The laws of this country do not prevent the strong from crushing the weak."

Woodrow Wilson, 1913

I never knew Woodrow Wilson, and he never knew me. But I wish that he had known me about a decade ago. Known me, and maybe whispered that bit of sage advice into my ear; he could have saved me a lot of trouble.

You see, I was *the weak* once… and the stupid, and the naïve. I had faith; faith in our government, faith in mankind, and worst of all, faith in our country's system of law and order. I believed that a system of justice - *our* system of justice - an adversarial process constructed of a confusing labyrinth of rules and terms: brief, arraignment, discovery, continuance, habeas corpus, lis pendens. I believed they would all be there for me when I needed them.

Instead, Justitia, the symbol of equity in our society, her eyes covered, a broadsword in one hand and a set of scales in the other, stood by mutely while I took a posterior augering. That's when it finally dawned on me that the expression, "justice is blind" was true. Justitia misses a hell of a lot of things. From that day on, I took the law into my own hands, and it felt really good.

* * *

Allow me to introduce myself, my name is John Sharp, but you can call me Jack, One Eyed Jack if you really want to be formal. Most of my friends call me Jack, although admittedly, it's a very short list of friends. My much longer list - a list of my enemies - mostly don't know my name, or where I live, or even what I look like. But I'm sure that it hasn't stopped them from referring to me from time to time in their own endearing terms: derogatory synonyms for private body parts, or base terms that suggest maternal incest. And one of the first names ever to be permanently inscribed on that long list of enemies, was that of my unscrupulous business partner. Without knowing it, he was the one who provided the nudge that thrust me into my current line of work.

About a decade ago, I had an idea to create a private label soda aimed at the youth market. The timing, I thought, couldn't have been better. All it would take was some capital, a lot of sweat, and some luck. But I couldn't do it all alone, and so I enlisted distributors to help me deliver the cases of product to various stores, markets, and snack bars.

One of these distributors who signed on with me decided that, after he had taken delivery of the product and sold a bunch of it, he would just skip the part about paying me. Enter here our fine legal system, which was of no help whatsoever.

You see, this distributor had all of the time in the world to deliver soda during normal working hours because he wasn't gainfully employed; he was on disability. Because of this nebulous employment status, if I went the traditional route and took him to small claims court, even if I prevailed, I wouldn't be able to collect on any judgment against him. He also had no assets, no savings, and a pile of bills as tall as the Empire State Building. A lesson here, dear reader, in picking business partners 101; make sure that they have something to lose. You wouldn't play poker against a man with no chips, would you?

Although he didn't have any hard assets, he did have a hole card he was trying to keep under wraps, a bogus lawsuit that claimed his knee was permanently damaged from a vehicle accident in which he was the "victim." Upon learning this juicy tidbit of information, I immediately contacted his ambulance-chasing attorney. I explained that soda cases are heavy, twenty-two pounds to be exact, and that anyone who could heft them and deliver them to stores all day could not possibly have a hopelessly ravaged anterior cruciate ligament (ACL), as he and his client were claiming.

The attorney angrily denounced me for engaging in extortion (which I was), and I fired right back that he and my erstwhile business partner were engaging in fraud (which they were). Once we got the semantics out of the way, I asked him if he was going to play ball and help me recover the money that was owed to me? Or, would he rather that I have this same conversation with Allstate Insurance, and he could watch helplessly as his thirty-three percent cut of the settlement vaporized right in front of his eyes?

The attorney recognized that I had both him and his client by the short-and-curlies, and so he readily cut me a deal; he would give me a lien against their future settlement in exchange for my silence on the whole affair. It was hush money, plain and simple, but I agreed. Two months later I had a check in my hand for the whole amount owed to me. That was when I realized that the justice system did work - *my* system of justice!

* * *

There are a lot of motels in the South Bay area of Los Angeles where I live and work, but only a handful of them can be considered viable candidates for what is termed, hosting, essentially a place to go have some great sex without your meddlesome spouse interfering. The Starlite Motel on Pacific Coast Highway has all the credentials needed to qualify as one of these fine establishments: it was on a heavily traveled street, it was nondescript, it offered day rates, and rooms could be rented with cash; thus no credit card trail. It is located in the working class town of Harbor City, and because its business model caters to this select clientele, it sees more landings and take-offs on an average day than nearby Los Angeles International Airport. Today, I hoped, would be no exception.

It was a Thursday afternoon, about two-thirty, and I was sitting in my minivan not far from the entrance of the Starlite, waiting for my next two targets to arrive. A high-definition video camera was mounted on a tripod bolted to the floor inside the van to take in all of the action. The camera fed a continuous stream to a laptop that was rendering real-time copies onto dual DVD burners. After I got enough damming footage of their escapades, a complimentary DVD would be placed onto the windshield of each of the participant's vehicles, along with instructions on how to avoid having the video find its way onto YouTube.com.

It was a warm day and the interior of the van was beginning to heat up. Beads of perspiration were forming on my forehead and brow. Thankfully, I didn't have to wait too much longer for the festivities to begin as the first of my unsuspecting marks arrived.

A man in a light-brown 2005 Buick LeSabre bounced into the potholed and battle-scarred parking lot of the Starlite, guiding his land-yacht into a space in front of one of the rooms. It was a plain vanilla car in a blasé color, unassuming in many ways - except for one; it had paper plates and a temporary registration in the back window.

To the unsuspecting eye, it might have appeared that the vehicle had been recently purchased from a car dealership, but I knew something was up; the paper plate was bulging out from the embossed characters on the real plate underneath it. It was an old trick and every cop was wise to it, but that didn't stop people from trying it from time to time. As soon as the boff-fest began inside the room, I'd rip off the paper plate so I could get the real numbers to run.

After a few seconds, a middle-aged man got out of the Buick and hurriedly began making his way to the office. He was about fifty years old, Caucasian, and pudgy, with a crop of short black hair that was going gray, and plastic-framed glasses. He was dressed in a short sleeve, pale yellow dress shirt, with brown slacks and brown shoes. The underarms and back of his shirt were soaked in sweat. He looked around nervously as he scampered quickly into the office to rent his room. He had a gold wedding band on the ring finger of his plump left hand.

Even though the most myopic of persons could have spotted Brown Shoes' unbridled display of guilt and shame from a mile away, I had been alerted to this specific upcoming rendezvous at the Starlite by none other than one of its own employees.

Under normal circumstances, motel employees could be counted on to be discreet and let what happened at their "No-Tell-Motel" stay there, but not Stan Halper. *Stan the man* was what I termed a "compromised" individual. You see, rather than follow the rules and studiously attend his college classes - as the terms of his wealthy grandmother's will dictated - Stan decided instead to spend his four years in academia engaged in a campaign of decadence and debauchery not seen since the Roman orgies.

Incorrectly assuming that he would only have to maintain his façade of the nose to the grindstone scholar until dear old gram kicked the bucket, Stan nevertheless found his tit in the ringer a few years later when she surprised everyone and continued to hang on in spite of her advanced age. And when the reality hit that he had no bona fide sheepskin to provide her when the demand came in, he had no choice but to turn to a forger who dealt in this form of document chicanery.

I know several forgers and other sundry purveyors of illicit goods, and this one was no different from the rest. When I went to lean on him about his dubious enterprise, he quickly cut a deal with me, and threw Stan and dozens of his other customers under the bus to save his own skin.

The cozy arrangement I made with the forger had so far netted me far in excess of what I could have made if I had simply squeezed him on his own. Stan was just one of a number of dissimulators who were on the hook to me for two hundred a month, as well as having to provide fresh intel about the comings and goings of the Starlite's philandering patrons. Oh, and Stan's grandma? She's doing just fine at ninety-one, and just joined a water aerobics class at the senior center.

Brown Shoes returned from the Starlite office a few minutes later with a cardkey clutched in his plump little hand. He was sweating profusely now and looked even more nervous - if that was even humanly possible. His eyes darted about wildly, and his head swiveled around like it was about to unscrew. I had him figured as a first timer when I first saw him walk to the office. Now I knew without a doubt that he was a guy who had never before pulled the trigger.

He made it back to his Buick without managing to have a massive coronary right in front of me. He hit the key fob and quickly climbed back into the driver's seat and waited. By now I had several minutes of good incriminating video, but the show was about to get better.

A brand new, off-white, 2016 Mercedes-Benz coupe rolled slowly into the lot. I knew that it was brand new because it had no rear plate and only a temporary registration paper taped up in the rear window. As soon as the fireworks began in the room, I'd have to get out and get the info off the temporary registration on the Benz. Boy, these two were going to make me work overtime today just to ID them.

I could see a female driver through the tinted glass, but I couldn't make out any features. As she made her way idling through the lot, she spotted Brown Shoes' Buick and flashed her headlights to let him know that his snack had arrived. Through the rear window of his car, I could see him nearly jump out of his skin.

The woman didn't pull her car into the spot next to him by the rooms - de rigueur for most co-conspirators. Instead, she backed her car into a parking slot one row over and directly behind him; an interesting break from custom, and for me, advantageous. From where she parked in relation to my van, I had a clean, unobstructed shot of the back end of her car, and into the vehicle's cabin.

She had the driver's side visor down, and fiddled around with the lighting knobs for a bit before she checked herself in the vanity mirror. After a few moments, she must have been satisfied with what she saw and exited the vehicle, leaving the visor in the lowered position.

I widened out and caught a good look at her - and she was a looker! She was in her late thirties or early forties, had a rocket body, and was dressed in an off-white skirt and jacket that was nearly a match for the color of her car. Her outfit was well tailored, with welted pockets and pleats, and it fit her lithe body well. Underneath the jacket she had on a silk blouse in a powder blue color. She had a satchel in the same off white shade, and her shoes were silver glitter sling-back pumps. She had no wedding ring on, and a necklace of pearls was the only jewelry I could spot on her.

She had a thick mane of red hair in a bob cut that curled forward to her jaw line. Sitting on top of her head, and raked jauntily to the right side, was a wide-brimmed derby hat that was the same color as her outfit. The hat was trimmed with a Sinamay flower of powder blue. Her eyes were covered with a pair of designer sunglasses.

I saw the taillights on the Mercedes flash, and Red made her way toward Brown Shoes' Buick and the rooms. In contrast to her soon-to-be playmate, she exhibited no anxiety or fear. She strode toward the Buick with the confident bearing of someone who had been in this rodeo before. In my years of experience, I had seen plenty of call girls, and I had her pegged instantly as a pro.

Brown Shoes got out of his car and they said a few words to each other before turning toward the bank of rooms. After just a couple of steps, Brown Shoes clumsily tripped on the low curb of the walkway. If this guy made it through today's dalliance in one piece, it would be a miracle.

I panned the camera and followed them as they entered their room. After the door closed, I was going to wait about a minute or so for things to get under way, and for them to become *in flagrante delicato*. In the meantime, I popped the key fob to automatically open the side door of the van to get some air.

Since Brown Shoes' partner in crime was a working girl, I debated on whether or not to take the time to get her info. But I had learned long ago that you can never have enough intelligence gathered. I doubted if I could lean on her too heavily, but it might come in handy some day if she ever wanted to cough up the names of some of her johns. After I got Brown Shoes' info, I'd snap a picture of the Mercedes' temporary registration so I could trace it. I had my phone in my hand, and the van door was the process of opening, when I caught some movement out of the corner of my eye. The door to the room opened up and Red stepped out, closing it quietly behind her.

Then she began heading toward her car - fast.

TWO

I shook my head, wondering how many times I had seen this tragicomedy play out before. A neophyte like Brown Shoes decides he's going to take the plunge and sow his wild oats. He finds an ad for escorts in the local paper, makes contact, negotiates a price, and sets up a liaison for what he figures is going to be the most mind-blowing sex of his life. Instead, he finds himself standing naked in the middle of an empty motel room, several hundred dollars lighter, and a whole lot wiser. Red had just ripped him off.

A pro told me once that the standard trick was to tell the guy that he smelled and he needed to clean up if she was going to go "around the world" with him. Not wanting to miss out on any of the E-ticket rides at this amusement park, the fool readily agrees. And while he's busy in the shower lathering himself up, she grabs his wallet and make tracks out the door before he even knows what happened. You get your fee, plus whatever extra cash he had on him. And if you want to, you could sell his ID and credit cards on the street for a couple of more bucks. Not a bad payday for keeping your legs closed.

Moving at a brisk but not suspicious pace, Red made it to the Mercedes in just a few seconds. She climbed in, started the car and peeled out of the parking lot faster than she had arrived. She turned right onto Pacific Coast Highway with nary a look and took off with a squeal of tires. I heard a chorus of angry car horns as several vehicles probably had to stop or swerve to avoid hitting her. But she didn't care if they honked or not; she was a woman who knew where she was going.

I returned my attention to Brown Shoes' room and waited for several minutes for him to finally emerge. When he did, he burst through the door and glared wildly out to the parking lot toward where Red's car had been parked, hoping desperately he could still catch her. He had a better chance of catching a greased Cheetah.

His hair was wet and dripping, and his yellow shirt was unbuttoned and draped loosely over his brown slacks. Several wet spots were evident on his rumpled clothes. He looked back and forth from one end of the parking lot to the other, hoping that she had just moved her car. Forget it pal; she played you for a sucker. Report your credit and ATM cards as lost, and start getting your story straight for your wife.

Resigned that he had been had, he started walking languidly toward his car, leaving the door to the room agape. It was then that I noticed he had a piece of paper in his hand. He looked down at it sadly and his face twisted up in a grimace. Had Red left him a nice note to rub salt in the wounds? That was a new one on me.

I activated the key fob to close the side door on the van. Without having his plate number, I knew that at some point I would be taking up a tail of Brown Shoes, and I didn't want any vehicle logistics to slow me down. Since they no longer served any purpose, I also shut down the video camera, and stealthily disconnected and stowed the laptop. I did, however, activate the dash cam I used when I tailed someone. The things it would pick up, that I would be too distracted to see as I drove, was amazing.

Brown Shoes popped the locks on his Buick and climbed in. He started the car just as I climbed into the front seat of the van. I started my engine and waited. Before long, I saw his brake lights and then his backup lights as he shifted the vehicle into reverse. He didn't pull away though and instead sat there, re-reading the note in his hand.

C'mon guy. Quit torturing yourself and just move on.

Finally, he backed out, then shifted the car into drive and drove towards the exit at the same unhurried pace. He turned left onto Pacific Coast Highway. As soon as I saw the rear quarter panel of his car disappear around the corner, I threw the shift lever of the van into drive and took off after him.

The game was afoot!

* * *

The vehicle I used for these operations was a midnight-blue 2010 Chrysler Town and Country minivan. The vehicle was courtesy of Otto's Autos in nearby Wilmington. They carry its title and the insurance on their dealer inventory list. It wasn't a "loaner" vehicle because I was having a tune-up done on my regular car, and Otto was no friend of mine. In fact, he was just one of several crooked used car dealers who were on my "enemies" list. Otto had earned that exalted distinction because he also just so happened to be one of the many dealers who seized on a unique opportunity when Mother Nature threw it his way.

If you remember Hurricane Sandy and all of the devastation it wrought, you may also remember seeing images of cars submerged underwater and damaged by the ensuing storm surge and flood. All told, there were an estimated quarter of a million cars that suffered damage as a result of Sandy, and those cars did not just disappear into the Bermuda Triangle.

Instead, these "flood cars" were adroitly purchased by shady wholesalers. The wholesalers would then work with equally crooked motor vehicle department operatives to *wash* the "salvage" titles clean. And good old Otto, a man who never missed a deal when it came his way, quickly capitalized on the distressed vehicles, and had them detailed and sparkling on his lot faster than you can say, "free floor mats."

After I got the goods on Otto, I offered him one of my standard wanton used car dealer contracts. In exchange for $300 a month sent to my re-mailing service in Texas, *and* unlimited use of any of his heaps, he could continue to count on my taciturnity. He could hardly wait to close the deal.

I caught up to Brown Shoes' Buick heading westbound on Pacific Coast Highway after a few minutes, and fell in about three cars behind and one lane over from him. He was in the number two lane and I was in number one. The traffic was moderate at this time of the day, but it would be picking up soon as kids got out of school and people left work.

Since I didn't want to miss anything, I double-checked that the dash cam was functioning. If I was incredibly lucky, and Brown Shoes hadn't affixed the paper plate properly, it might fly off and I would have all the info I needed.

Still heading west on Pacific Coast Highway, we passed through the bedroom community of Lomita before veering slightly north toward the city of Torrance. To our right was the Torrance Municipal Airport, named Zamperini Field in honor of the inspiring World War II hero.

I moved into the number two lane occupied by Brown Shoes' Buick and closed the gap to just one car between us. He was driving at a sedate speed and we were moving along nicely. The car separating us changed lanes, and now I was directly behind him. Then I noticed that the bottom of the paper plate had begun to flutter, exposing fragments of the characters. I crossed my fingers that Lady Luck would hitch a ride with me today.

We passed through the upper middle-class areas of South Torrance and then Brown Shoes put his left blinker on and moved back over into the number one lane. I cut over into the number three lane, dropped back several cars, and then made my way back over into the number one lane.

Tailing a vehicle properly, by yourself, without detection, *and* without losing it, was akin to an art form. You had to balance the competing priorities of staying close enough to maintain visual contact, while still not arousing any suspicion from the target vehicle. Add to this, all of the wildcards: signal lights, a giant truck blocking you, road construction, police or emergency vehicle activity, and it became a real juggling act.

After a few moments, the left turn signal on the Buick began to flash again. He slowed down and pulled into the left-hand turn lane at Palos Verdes Boulevard. I couldn't help but break into a smile. Despite his plain vanilla car and drab wardrobe, old Brown Shoes might just be loaded. Palos Verdes Boulevard takes you straight up into the Palos Verdes Peninsula. The peninsula, which rises from the Pacific Ocean to over 1450 feet above sea level, is home to several cities: Palos Verdes Estates, Rancho Palos Verdes, Rolling Hills, and Rolling Hills Estates, all of which are considered the most affluent cities in the South Bay area. "PV" or "The Hill," as it is referred to by locals, is the realm of private country clubs, top-notch schools, equestrian trails, and stunning ocean views, all of which are available to anyone who has a measly $1.5 million to plunk down for the median home price. As I liked to say when I found out that one of my targets lived in PV; "There's gold in them-thar hills!"

I slowed down enough to agitate a driver behind me into passing me, and getting in between myself and the Buick - which is exactly what I wanted him to do. At the intersection with Malaga Cove, Brown Shoes veered to the right onto Palos Verdes Drive West, and toward Palos Verdes Estates. It was a single lane here and getting breezy, but I could tell, as we worked our way through the curves in the road, that the paper faux plate was starting to sail up a little higher and reveal more of the characters underneath.

But I still couldn't see enough to decipher them positively, so I had to stay on the tail.

We continued on Palos Verdes Drive West, climbing farther and farther up the hill, until the Douglas Cut where the road became divided. Brown Shoes turned right at the intersection and continued down onto Paseo Del Mar. Beyond us lay the stunning vista of the Pacific Ocean and Catalina Island. Seeing the island twenty-six miles off in the distance, I instinctively began humming the famous song.

From my position directly behind him, I had a good view of Brown Shoes through the back window of the Buick. He appeared to be getting more and more agitated the farther he drove. I could see the silhouette of his shoulders as they rose and fell, as if he was struggling to breathe. His free hand came up and he repeatedly wiped his forehead. Then…

Oh shit!

At the intersection of Paseo Del Mar and Chiswick Road, he reached down with his right hand and uncoupled his seat belt. To our right was an open expanse of land, probably one of the last undeveloped pieces of real estate left in the area. The dirt lot was barren and sloped down gently for a hundred feet or so before disappearing at the edge of the bluff. The drop off these cliffs was steep and deadly, ending several hundred feet below on the bolder-strewn coastline.

Brown Shoes turned sharply to the right and accelerated. The big Buick bounced up over the low curb and onto the lot. I saw the rear wheels spin up a spray of dirt as he floored it. The car fishtailed briefly, but then he corrected it. He aimed the car straight for the cliff.

I watched in horror as he sailed off and disappeared.

THREE

I slammed on the brakes and the van came to an abrupt stop just a short distance away from where Brown Shoes had gone up and over the curb. The concrete face of the curb had black scuff marks where the tires had hit. Through the window, I could hear some commotion to my left. I turned to see a middle-aged couple standing on the opposite sidewalk holding a small dog on a leash. The woman had a look of horror on her face and was screaming, the man had a cell phone to his ear. I rolled down the window.

"Oh my God!" the women cried out. "Did you see that?"

I didn't respond other than to ask, "Are you calling 911?"

The man, still with the phone to his ear, looked up at me and nodded.

"Okay," I said. "I'm going to go get a rope at my house."

I gunned the van and pulled away as fast as I could. 911 was already being called, and I didn't need to get caught up in this and have to explain to the cops:

1. Why was I was driving up here?
2. Why was I driving a loner from Otto's Autos?
3. And why, pray tell, did I have a camera mounted on a tripod in the back seat?

Besides that, I knew the area and I knew the odds. Since it was the highest point around with sheer cliffs, PV was popular for suicides, both vehicular and pedestrian. Only twenty percent of the people attempting them ever survived. Brown Shoes was dead. He disconnected his seat belt, and even with the airbags deploying, they were only good to about thirty-five mph. From this height, he would have hit at over sixty. The floorboards would have crumpled up into the passenger compartment and cleaved his legs right out of his pelvis, severing the femoral arteries in the process. The car could have also flipped and landed upside down, the roof caving in on him. If the tide was in, the car would have filled with water and he would have drowned.

I drove to Cloyden Road and turned left to get the heck out of Dodge. I turned left again at Palos Verdes Drive West and started heading back down the hill the same way I had come. Heading up, in the opposite direction from me, a police car and several paramedic units were racing to the hopeless scene. Their lights were flashing and sirens screamed as they went by me.

I pulled my Blackphone out of the holster. To the average person, it looked like a run-of-the-mill Android phone, but it used a custom-built Android operating system called *PrivatOS*. The operating system essentially closes all of the “backdoors” which are usually left open on major mobile operating systems. It was ultra secure and allowed me to make either un-encrypted or encrypted calls. To another Blackphone, it would perform peer-to-peer calls.

I said, “Dial Tiffany. Encryption on.”

She answered after three rings.

“Hey baby,” she said brightly. “What’s up?”

“What are you doing right now?” I asked.

“Just puttering around the house until I have to leave for the club. Why? What’s wrong?”

“Nothing’s wrong,” I lied.

“Bullshit Jack,” she said. “I can tell. Now tell me what’s wrong.”

“I’ll tell you in a bit. Do you have time to meet me at The Sea Sprite for a drink?”

“Sure.”

“Okay. I’ll see you there in about twenty minutes.”

“Drive safely,” she said cautiously, then added, “I love you.”

“Love you, too,” I said before terminating the call.

FOUR

The beach areas of Redondo, Hermosa, and Manhattan had plenty of watering holes. Most of them tended to be upscale hipster joints with loud music, boisterous crowds, and overpriced drinks. Only a few of the old relic dive bars remained. The Sea Sprite was one of these establishments. Located in Hermosa, directly on The Strand at the base of what used to be known as Pier Avenue, The Sea Sprite had been built around the same time a member of the Whig party had last occupied the White House - and it hadn't changed much since then. That was just fine with me. I didn't feel hip or trendy right now…or even clean. I felt dirty; and The Sprite was just the spot to go to when you felt soiled.

I had only been in The Sprite a couple of times before in my life, but stepping in after a several year absence was analogous to missing your favorite soap opera for a season or two; nothing ever changed, and the characters were the same as they ever were. The interior was dark, and like many practiced boozers, I knew to let my eyes adjust before venturing in too far.

A long curved bar took up a good quarter of the floor space, and surrounding it were several booths, as well as individual tables that looked out through tinted glass windows to the sand and surf beyond. Besides serving generous drinks that tested the limits of human liver capacity, The Sea Sprite also catered to those wishing to meet an early demise in a more gastronomic manner. The flamethrower chili was the special today, along with a quadruple-stuffed bacon cheeseburger known as "The Widow-Maker."

After my eyes adjusted, I stepped over to the bar, found a stool, and ordered a vodka tonic. There were just a handful of people there, but they were the diehard regulars whose consumption habits could keep a place like that afloat all on their own. One of them, an aged matron who looked about as old as electricity, sat silently, three stools down from me.

She had dyed-brown hair, teased up high like a bald eagle's nest, on a large head that turned to study me as soon as I sat down. Her eyes were pale gray and rheumy. The skin on her face was sagging and mapped with the innumerable lines of someone who drank and smoked too much. Evidence to that conjecture sat in front of her on the bar: a crumpled pack of Virginia Slims and a highball glass with lipstick smudges around the rim. She piped up as soon as my drink arrived.

"Nice patch, honey," she croaked, referring to the snakeskin eye patch I wore.

"Hmmm," I mumbled, and took a big swallow of the vodka tonic, which was volatile enough to power a rocket into outer space.

"I said, nice patch, honey," she repeated in her rasp.

I turned to her. "I heard you," I said. "Thank-you."

I turned back to my drink and took a smaller sip this time.

"How'd you lose your eye, honey?" she asked.

I ignored her.

"I said, how'd you lose your eye honey?" she said with an insistent tone.

Finally, I had had enough and I spun around to her.

"Looking at an ugly, old hag," I said harshly. "And I've only got one left; so I better not take any chances!"

I picked up my drink and was striding away to one of the booths when she called out after me, "Ass-hole!"

"Making friends already, huh Jack?"

It was Tiffany, my girlfriend and a sight for sore eyes, or in my case, *eye*-singular.

I gave her a big kiss and a hug, and then motioned her into the booth.

We had been together for a little more than half a year, and we were very close, despite the bizarre manner in which our lives had been become connected over half a decade prior.

She was the trophy wife turned widow of Dr. Edwin Karch, a famously talented plastic surgeon from Beverly Hills. I had just started out in the blackmailing game several years prior, and Dr. Karch was one of my early targets. Even though he had the hot, nubile Tiffany to keep his libido satisfied, Karch could never seem to shake a fetish he had for young male prostitutes. I captured some nice video of him picking up a boy-toy in Hollywood and presented the goods to him at his office a couple of days later, along with a convenient payment plan to keep the tape hidden.

But rather than cement a nice long business relationship with me, the good doctor turned the tables by informing a client of his - a Russian mobster named Viktor Durov who was on the run and looking to have his identity changed - about my little scheme. The next thing I knew, I was kidnapped by the mobster and his thugs, and prepped for some free surgical work, courtesy of Dr. Karch. I woke up several hours later in the hills above Los Angeles, sans one of my peepers.

As much as I hated to, I had to give Durov credit for his style. He could have just as easily killed me to get me out of the way, but instead, he chose to make his point on a more poetic, albeit brutal level. He wanted me to be reminded all of my waking hours, of the mistake I made by sticking my nose into other people's business. In a way, the mobster and I were kindred spirits; I operated under the same philosophy. I could charge my targets a big one-time fee to keep quiet about their secrets and then just move on to the next one. Or, I could hack into their computers, steal all of their account passwords, and rob them blind.

But every month, when they sent off that envelope full of cash, I wanted them to be reminded about what they had done, who they had wronged, and how they tried to cheat at the game of life and got caught. Mine was the hair shirt they would have to wear for their indiscretions until they either got divorced, fired, audited by the IRS, or simply died. But I never wanted to drive anyone to suicide.

Dr. Karch died suspiciously a couple of years after my initial encounter with him, most likely at the hands of the mobster himself. I thought the whole thing was over between us, but a chance encounter with Durov's henchmen a half a year ago drew me right back into his corrupt and violent world. Trying to juggle too many balls in the air, I ended up orchestrating a very clever double cross against him, which only served to amplify his already significant ire with me.

In the meantime, Tiffany had discovered that most of her and her late husband's wealth had been the financial equivalent of smoke and mirrors. And by the time all of the dust had settled and the bills were paid, she ended up destitute and reduced to taking menial jobs to scrape by. But, she was also the only possible connection between the expired doctor and the mobster. I needed to understand who my malefactor was, and she needed to see if she had any remaining wealth, so we teamed up to our mutual benefit. She ended up saving my life, and we fell in love and moved in together. The disposition of Durov though, remained a mystery.

A waitress appeared at our table from out of nowhere and Tiffany ordered a glass of chardonnay.

"So what's going on, Jack?" Tiffany asked, as soon as the waitress stepped away.

"I just watched a man kill himself," I said flatly.

"What! How?"

I took another swallow of my rocket fuel and grimaced.

"He and some escort setup a slam dance at a motel in Harbor City," I started. "The man had phony paper plates covering up his real ones, and the pro was driving a brand new Benz, sans plates. I got the video of them pulling in and going into the room together and - "

The waitress arrived with Tiffany's wine and set it down. She looked at my glass and cocked an eyebrow. Without knowing it, I had drained all of the contents.

"Sure," I said. "But you could ask him to make it lighter?"

"I can try," she said doubtfully, as she scooted away.

"So they get into the room," I continued. "And before I know it, she's outside and heading to her car."

Tiffany took a dainty sip on her wine. "So what happened?"

"She ripped him off," I said easily. "It happens all the time."

The waitress returned with my drink.

"Happy hour," she said. "Twelve bucks."

I stuck a twenty into her hand and waved her on. She smiled; that made her hour happy too.

Tiffany took another sip of her wine and looked over the rim of her glass at me with her emerald green eyes. Her face was narrow with high cheekbones, and she had a wide, full mouth with straight white teeth. She had a nose that turned up at the tip, just enough to be cute, and her hair was blond and hung down just past her shoulders. Recently she had traded her center part for bangs. It was a nice effect, and I was awestruck at times just how beautiful she was, and how a lug like me had ended up with her.

"Whoa!" someone at the bar bellowed out, and Tiffany and I turned toward the sound. On the TV over the bar, the local news had been turned on. On the screen was an aerial shot of the rugged Palos Verdes coastline. The camera zoomed tight into the center of the screen, and there was Brown Shoes' Buick. It was upside down on the roof and half-submerged in the water. As I had correctly estimated, the front end of the car had been pushed in about three feet, jamming the engine and transmission into the cabin of the car, killing him instantly. Below the shot of the car was a footer that read: *Breaking News: Car plunges off cliff in Palos Verdes.*

I gestured to the screen with my drink. "That's him," I said.

"Oh my God, Jack!" Tiffany said. "And you saw it happen? How?"

I told her the whole story of my tail of Brown Shoes in his car, which took most of my drink to tell. When I was done, Tiffany took a dainty sip of her wine, and considered what I had recited to her.

"And you don't think he knew you were tailing him?" she asked.

"No," I said emphatically. "No way. No evasive maneuvers, no changing lanes, speeding up. Hell, I don't think he even looked in his rearview mirror."

"Do you think that the note had anything to do with it?" Tiffany asked.

"I don't know," I admitted. "Maybe. I'd sure like to see what it said."

Before long, we had both finished our drinks. The waitress came by again and I took another vodka tonic. Tiffany had a show to do so she passed on another glass of wine.

One of the conditions of her marriage to Dr. Karch was that she would give up her career as a jazz singer. Whether it was to keep her away from the solicitations of other men, play sugar daddy to her, or what, I didn't know. But her career had just been taking off when they got together, and she always felt robbed that she had to give it up. Since we had been together, she had begun to resurrect it and was doing quite well. She had a steady schedule of gigs at prominent clubs, like the one she was playing that night, and she was scheduled to go on a ten city tour in just a couple of weeks. I would be lost and lonely without her, but I promised myself never to stand in the way of her dreams as her late husband had.

She glanced at the Cartier Baignoire watch I had given her for our six month anniversary, and said, "Sorry, Jack. I've got to run off and finish getting beautiful for the show."

I said to her with a wink, "You are finished."

She got up and slung her purse over her shoulder. She smiled and bent over to kiss me softly on the lips. It was the best feeling I had all day.

"Not too many of those," she warned, gesturing to my drink. Then she turned her attention to the TV screen. By now, the scene at the cliffs was in full force. A Los Angeles County Sheriff's rescue team had been lowered by helicopter to the base of the cliffs and three men were in the water trying to gain access to the cabin of the car. The crashing waves made it extremely difficult, as well as dangerous. A lifeguard boat sat anchored just outside of the surf line. The cliffs above were filled with fire trucks, police cruisers, and throngs of onlookers.

"Just forget about this tonight, Jack," Tiffany said. "It's not your fault. You didn't get his plate number, and I know it's driving you crazy to not have any details to unravel this. In a day or so, they'll have his name out, and you can go ahead and try to make sense of it. Until then, just go home and relax."

I stared at the TV, the news anchors back in the studio were inset in a picture in picture, and babbling on with what was nothing more than speculation. They knew nothing at the moment. I knew more than anybody did at this point, and it was still next to nothing.

"You're right," I said to Tiffany. "I'll finish my drink, and then go home and just relax."

She smiled a knowing smile and then said, "No you won't. As soon as I leave, you'll be on the hunt. And you'll stay on the hunt all night if you have to. When something like this happens, you're like a pit bull that gets something in its mouth and won't let it go."

I smiled back at her. "Boy, am I glad I don't have to go toe-to-toe with you."

She kissed me again, and then it was her turn to wink. "We'll go toe-to-toe when I get home later Jack - if you know what I mean."

Tiffany turned and left before I could come up with a good comeback, which I probably couldn't have anyway.

And as soon as she was out the door, I did exactly what she said I would do; I pulled out my phone and began the hunt.

FIVE

Having already synched the videos from both my tripod camera and the dash cam to my phone, I navigated to the folder I titled "Brownshoes" and opened it. I skipped the video from the scene at the motel, and instead went straight to the dash cam footage and the part I was looking for; Brown Shoes' bogus paper license plate fluttering in the breeze.

Most of the characters on the real plate underneath had been exposed - at least the bottom third or so of them - and I wondered if there was enough of the plate to ID it. I had a guy working at the Department of Motor Vehicles I was leaning on. He could do some referencing based upon the car's make, model, color, and year. And assuming Brown Shoes was from the local area, maybe he could narrow it down for me. But it was too late in the day for that, the DMV was closing in just ten minutes. I did have another arrow in my quiver. I had a computer hacker who I used from time to time who had access to various government and business databases.

His name was Zahid Shukla, and he was a brilliant software engineer from Pakistan. How we had come to know each other had been a fluke. I had unknowingly discovered the same piece of damming information as someone else who was trying to leverage it against him.

Zahid's student visa had expired several years earlier, but he had managed to somehow wriggle his way into a job at an upstart company developing anti-malware software for smartphones. His boss, a succubus by the name of Ed "Fast Eddie" Santos, was fully aware of Zahid's dubious immigration status, and decided to use it to his own advantage. He wanted Zahid to develop malware on the side that would actually defeat the very same product the company was developing and distributing, essentially, playing both sides of the fence.

Zahid wanted to rebuff his boss' demands, but by now had a wife and a family, and he did not want to see all of them deported. When I coincidentally interrogated him about the very same issue, he spilled his guts about how Santos was already squeezing him. I decided to come to his rescue, if he would promise to help me with any future computer issues, such as hacking into other systems, while keeping mine secure.

Zahid agreed to the deal, but Santos turned out to be a tougher nut to crack than most. Unlike most of my targets, Fast Eddie had no downside risks as far as relationships went. His few friends were as scheming as he was, his wives had all divorced him years ago, his siblings were estranged from him, and his kids hated his guts. In short, he had nothing to lose, or so I thought.

Every man has a weakness, a chink in his armor, and it should have come as no surprise to me that a miscreant like Santos came in the form of his insatiable appetite for games of chance. He had an addiction to gambling, and made almost weekly trips to Las Vegas.

Through my guidance, and with Zahid's sock-puppetry, we created a bogus offshore virtual gambling site that was licensed through the Kahnawake Tribe Gaming Commission in Quebec, Canada. The site would auto-generate virtual players who would join into games and lose money, with the "winnings" funneling back into an offshore bank account that was ostensibly in Santos' name. Santos had no knowledge or affiliation with the online casino or bank account we had created, and the virtual money that was skimmed off, was simply cycled back through as wagers by the next round of fantasy suckers in the game. In practice, it was the perfect zero-sum equation and no money was either won or lost. But it didn't look that way to an outsider, and anyone with a modicum of knowledge about scams could see that the game was rigged from a mile away. By all appearances, Fast Eddie Santos was hauling in huge profits from his unsuspecting pigeons.

The traditional casinos loathed any competition in general and offshore virtual sites even more. And any inkling that Zahid's boss was connected with the site - especially if it was crooked - would instantly make him persona non grata in Sin City. To a diehard player like Fast Eddie Santos, this was the equivalent of a death sentence. Presented with the incriminating evidence by none other than yours truly, he quickly folded his hand like he couldn't even come up with openers. Zahid now had a permanent work visa, a new job, and he and his family were on the road to US citizenship.

I launched the video chat app on my phone, dialed Zahid, and in a few moments he connected to me on his computer. On the screen on my phone, I could see that he was balancing a toddler on his lap.

"Hello, Jack," I heard Zahid say. "How are you?"

"Fine, Zahid," I said. "Just fine. Is that Aaima on your lap?"

"Yes. She is getting big, isn't she?"

His voice had the musical, lilting quality like many from the Indian sub-continent. It was nice to hear, and it was nice to see him with a growing family.

"She sure is," I said.

Zahid turned and said something to someone off-screen. In a few moments, I saw another set of hands, female, reaching for Aaima and lifting her off Zahid's lap. My guess was the hands were Zahid's wife, Parveen. He turned back to his monitor, and I heard the plaintive wail of a child in the background.

"What can I do for you, Jack?" Zahid asked.

"I'm trying to ID the owner of a car," I said. "I know the make, model, and year, but I only have a partial on the plate. Do you think you can help me?"

"Sure. California plates?"

"My guess is yes based on the background and character colors of the plate. Are you in the California DMV database?"

"Yes."

"Okay good. I have some video footage that I can send you, but like I said, it only shows a partial. The driver tried covering up the real plate with some paper plates, but they were fluttering as he drove, and you can make out the bottom third of most of the characters."

"Not a problem, Jack," Zahid said breezily. "I have an LPR program that I can modify to give me probabilities and possible combos. Such as, the bottom of an oval on the plate could represent a "C" an "O" or a "U". I'll have all of the possible combinations crunched, and then it will be a simple matter of matching a combination with the specific make, model, and year of car. Then we can find the registered owner."

The man was a bona fide genius and a godsend to me. I knew what an LPR program was; it stood for "license plate reader." Police departments had forward and side-looking cameras connected to a computer that could read license plates as a cruiser rolled down the street or through a parking lot. The computer was linked in real time to a database back at the headquarters. If any of the plates were tied to stolen cars, or if the vehicle had outstanding warrants, the software would alert the officer who would then take appropriate action. Zahid could tweak the computer software to enable it to list possible letters or numbers based on the fragments I had captured in the video.

"Thanks Zahid. Great. I have a video I'm going to send you from a tail of the car. It's a 2005 Buick LeSabre by the way."

"No problem Jack, send away. I'll get on it right away and get back to you."

I began forwarding the video to Zahid's secure e-mail.

"Thanks, Zahid," I said. "Say hi to Parveen for me."

"Will do, Jack. Signing off."

The display on my phone went dark, then returned to the home screen. With nothing else to do in the meantime, I drained what was left of my drink and started to head out of the Sea Sprite. I paused one last time to look at the TV over the bar to catch any updates about the rescue operation. Someone had already changed the channel and the patrons were yelling at hockey players battling on the ice. Already, everyone had forgotten.

* * *

I was just pulling into the garage at our house when my phone went off; it was Zahid calling me back. I put the minivan into park and answered it before I switched off the engine.

"Hello Zahid."

"Hi Jack. I have your plate number and registration."

"Thanks. That was fast."

"Piece of cake as you Americans say, Jack," Zahid laughed. "Like I said, I simply decoded the plate based upon the fragments you captured in the video. The software came up with seventeen different possible combinations, but only one of them belongs to a light-brown 2005 Buick, LeSabre."

"So who owns it, Zahid?"

"Not who, Jack. What."

"What do you mean?"

"The car is registered to the God's Way Church in Redondo Beach."

SIX

I sat there silently, stunned by the gravity of what Zahid had just told me. When I didn't say anything for a few moments, he must have thought the call had dropped.

"Jack…Jack…are you there?"

"Oh, yeah. Sorry Zahid. I was just lost in thought. Thanks again for your work on this."

"No problem Jack. I'll send you an e-mail with all of the specifics. Let me know if you need anything else."

"Will do. Thanks."

I terminated the call, switched off the car, and headed into the house. Before the engine had even cooled, I was logged onto my computer and digging for dirt.

* * *

In the world of intelligence gathering, there are several disciplines: HUMINT (human intelligence), SIGINT (signal intelligence), and FININT (financial intelligence). But the starting point for most intelligence collection is OSINT, or open source intelligence. Simply defined, this is any data or intelligence that is acquired through open source or public media, like newspaper and magazine articles, TV reporting, or in today's connected world, the Internet.

Like many modern houses of worship, the God's Way Church had a website. And like many of the same ilk, it had information about the church, a schedule of services, a special events calendar, and a listing of its leadership and staff. Most vital of all to the God's Way spiritual engine, the site had a donation page, complete with a PayPal portal, as well as a gentle hint about tithing from II Corinthians 9:7-8.

Some parts of the website were apparently under construction, and a disclaimer said as much and asked for the flock's patience in navigating it. Thankfully, the leadership directory on the site was still intact, and that's where I mined my first piece of gold.

Brown Shoes' real name was Roy Mentzer, or Pastor Roy. He was the Senior Pastor, and the founder of God's Way Church. The institution, like so many of its kind, had a tragic genesis and traced its roots to 1999 when Roy - homeless, addicted to methamphetamine, and hitting rock bottom - was spared a life of eternal damnation when he was fortuitously saved by Jesus. He got clean, and immediately set upon a lifelong quest to save other souls adrift in a sea of evil temptation.

From its humble beginnings in a converted gas station in South Los Angeles, the ministry had grown over the past decade and a half to its present size. There were over three thousand members, and God's Way had a campus with three buildings comprising close to sixty-thousand square feet of space. The campus sat on four acres of prime real estate in Redondo Beach. It included a cafe and a bookstore, a children's ministry, a teen ministry, a main sanctuary that seated over two-thousand, and a separate children's sanctuary that could hold over five-hundred tiny souls. In addition to the website, they also had a Facebook page, a Twitter feed, and a YouTube channel which carried videos of past sermons.

I poured through the website and took mental notes more than anything else. It was pretty much standard fluff for these places. Navigating to Google, I found pretty much the same information in most of the online articles that I read about God's Way and Pastor Roy. Now that I had a starting point, it was time to change gears.

I checked my watch and saw that it was already past ten o'clock. Tiffany's show had been going on for over an hour. I picked up my phone and sent her a text asking her how she was, how the gig was going, and told her that I missed her. I ended the message with *XOXO* and an emoticon of a yellow face pursing its lips to kiss. Then I hit send.

By now, the drinks from The Sea Sprite had worn off and I was getting hungry. I went to the refrigerator and spied the offerings: leftover Chicken Marsala, some ham and cheese quiche, a piece of rib eye steak and part of a baked potato, some macaroni and cheese, (I had no idea where it came from), and some Chicken Florentine Lasagna. I settled on the lasagna, sectioned a piece to put it on a plate, and then popped it into the microwave. While my food was busy absorbing radiation, I open a beer, took a swig, and pondered Brown Shoes' demise.

It was a tragic end to a life that had held so much promise. Unlike many addicts, Pastor Roy was able to turn the corner on his own life. Besides that, he had also dedicated the rest of it to saving others. Now, he was probably lying naked on a stainless steel table in a coroner's office, his mangled body set to be dissected and probed like a frog in a high school biology lab.

I heard the microwave shut down and begin bleating its annoying little chime. I pulled out the plate, grabbed some utensils and a paper napkin, and returned to my computer. With the open source info on Pastor Roy exhausted, it was time to do some deep data-mining.

* * *

After losing my eye to Viktor Durov and his lackey surgeon, Dr. Edwin Karch, several years prior, I was understandably traumatized and had decided that I should go straight and hang up my blackmailing spurs. To that end I took up employment at insurance company as a fraud investigator. After all of my years digging up the dirt in people's lives it seemed an obvious fit, and I did very well at it.

In fact, I did a little *too* well to suit my boss' fancy, who thought that my success at sniffing out scams was eclipsing her talents, and that it could possibly lead to the short-circuiting of her career. Her name was Melinda Harrigan, and she quickly embarked on a campaign to, if not outright discredit me, at least erect some sort of a bulwark to defend her own position against my adroitness.

She soon began assigning me the dog cases; ones that were either impossible to prove - and therefore would suck up all of my time - or were so blatantly obvious in their chicanery that a blind man could see the hanky-panky from a mile away. I realized immediately what was going on, and I went to her about it to complain.

She was all denial and protestations, and over the next several months we butted heads constantly. Finally, I had enough of being her personal boot-scraper and resorted to my old tricks. I began to dig up the dirt on my scheming boss - and it didn't take long to have a snow shovel's worth.

Our company had an obviously bogus claim against it from a person who said he had injured his back by slipping on some spilled OJ in a supermarket. The claimant was a very good-looking man in his mid-thirties, *and* he was single. I smelled a rat, but my scheming boss only smelled Aqua Velva.

At forty years old and twice divorced, Melinda Harrigan was desperate to sink her talons into some "Y" chromosomes lest the biological parade passed her by. She began dating him secretly and thought she was going to get away with it. Then one day, good old One Eyed Jack paid a visit to her office and dropped a pile of muck the size of Mount Everest onto her desk.

Realizing that dating anyone the company was investigating was a terminable offense, and presented with the irrefutable evidence: photos, videos, phone, and text records - she launched a charm offensive the magnitude of which I had never seen before. She offered me my own choice of cases, a new office, a raise, and a promotion - *anything* to save her neck from the chopping block.

The whole experience had been ugly and unnecessary had she only played nice, but it also was exhilarating and had taught me one important lesson; I loved my former profession and I missed it dearly. So instead of accepting all of the perks she offered me to save her skin, I told her I was resigning, and that I wanted three month's severance pay *and* to retain access to the company's investigative website known as Emperium. It was a service used by investigative journalists and insurance fraud investigators, and it would serve me well when I made my prodigal return to the world of professional extortion. My former boss couldn't accept my resignation fast enough.

* * *

I took a bite of the lasagna, washed it down with a swallow of beer, and logged onto the site. After I was in, I entered the name *Roy Mentzer* and *Los Angeles* in the appropriate search fields and came up with four hits. I scrolled down to the one that listed "minister" as the profession, clicked on it, and took another bite of my dinner.

It was here that the real story of Pastor Roy's life began to take shape. If open source intel was like looking at the trunk of a tree, the data the Emperium site yielded was akin to examining its rings under a microscope.

The late Pastor Roy was forty-eight years old, and was married. Apparently, in addition to cleaning up his act and doing a spiritual course correction in his life, he had found his soul mate in a young woman by the maiden name of Betty Callahan, current age, forty-four. The Mentzers had three children together: a boy Shaun David, age eleven, a girl Christina Rose, aged ten, and another boy, Colton Thomas, aged eight.

From what I could deduce based upon the information on the Emperium site, Betty Callahan had joined young Roy's ministry in approximately 2001, a couple of years after he had started it. They were married in 2003, and she quit her job as a paralegal not long after to assume her proper role of the obedient, stay at home mom - just as the scriptures dictated.

The Emperium site displayed only the driver's license photos for both Roy and Betty Mentzer, and no pictures of the children. I did a quick Google search for Roy Mentzer images and it steered me back to the God's Way Facebook page where someone had tagged photos of Roy, Betty, and several of the Mentzer children at various church events. The children looked to be the clean-cut, wholesome offspring of a man of the cloth, and Betty appeared to be a devoted, doting wife. It was a nice picture of a nice family, one that would now be testing the limits of their faith.

Before I navigated away, I "liked" the God's Way Facebook page.

I finished my dinner and my beer at about the same time I completed my basic perusal of the Mentzer family genealogy. Being the systematic person I am, I started my foray into other corners of their lives; legal, financial, and medical.

As I had expected, Roy Mentzer's early life, leading up to his discovery of Jesus, was a messy array of arrests and incarcerations. He was convicted several times for drug offenses, as well as residential and auto burglary, vagrancy, intoxication while in public, and an assault case where he pulled a knife on a fellow addict. Just as predictably, the time after his Christian rebirth painted an entirely different picture and the newly reformed Pastor Roy had no further scrapes with the law.

Since Betty Mentzer (née Callahan) had once held a job as a paralegal, I expected to see no criminal record for her. However, I was surprised by what I found.

Betty Callahan did indeed have a rap sheet, although it was tame compared to her husband's. She had a shoplifting arrest, as well as a drug conviction for pot, a DUI offense, and one charge for selling stolen goods that was later dropped. All of the offenses were prior to her meeting Roy and joining his ministry, and most were from when she was in her early twenties. It wasn't easy to get a certificate as a paralegal if you had a criminal record. But then again, Betty Callahan could have done it through an online course, and she could have found a sympathetic employer who would hire her.

The Mentzer children had no juvenile records, and quite possibly walked the straight and narrow. I could have gone back to Facebook, but the Mentzer children were too young to have accounts as they were all under thirteen. Instead, I delved into the family's financial records, hoping to unearth some dirt that might shed light on Roy's untimely demise. I was disappointed with what I found, and realized that based on my batting average that day, it was a good thing I never ran off to join the carnival to guess people's weights and ages for a living.

Since they had both gotten their lives together and forged a new path forward, the Mentzers had cleaned up whatever lingering debts they had, and appeared to be living within their means. Roy earned an unexceptional annual salary from God's Way of $87,000 but that didn't tell the whole story. As part of his compensation for being the lead Pastor, the family occupied a modest home in nearby Torrance that was owned by the church. And, as Zahid had discovered, the Buick Roy was driving when he took his plunge, was also owned by the church. The Mentzers did have one other vehicle that they owned personally: a 2012 Chevrolet Traverse that they were close to paying off. Their credit card debt was low, and their score with Equifax was 742. No juicy tidbits there.

I finally turned to the medical records and decided, just for grins and giggles, to start with Colton, the youngest of the Mentzer children, and work my way up. It didn't take long to go through all of the kids, and other than the usual childhood diseases such as measles and chickenpox, they seemed to be reasonably healthy. With nothing more to discover regarding the children, I moved up the family totem and was surprised by what I found.

Just like her minor criminal record, Mrs. Mentzer was once again the wildcard, albeit one she had dealt to her. After having two vaginal births and one cesarean (with Colton), she was diagnosed with ovarian cancer in 2009 and underwent a radical hysterectomy at the tender age of thirty-eight. She had regular checkups since her surgery, and seemed to be in the clear as far as any metastasization or recurrence.

Last but not least was Pastor Roy. Other than being mildly overweight and taking medication for high cholesterol, he was as healthy as a horse - at least as healthy as a dead horse could be.

My phone chimed that I had a text from Tiffany. She was in her car and on her way home. ETA: one hour.

I leaned away from the computer and rubbed my eyes. It was almost two-thirty in the morning. I could continue digging further, but after the events of today, I didn't have any energy left, and I thought it would just be a waste of time anyway. I didn't find any smoking gun, nor did I think I would if I continued mining. The answer wasn't going to be uncovered in the virtual world of data, financial records, court documents, or annual checkups, it was going to be found somewhere else.

The late Pastor Roy Mentzer had no dire financial issues, no terminal disease, and no other obvious reasons which drive a man to suicide. Yet, less than twelve hours ago, he did the deed with the zeal of a man who had no other escape. Had he been so embarrassed that he had been played for a sucker and gotten ripped off? Or was he so racked by guilt for trying to have sex outside of his marriage that he couldn't live with himself? And, just what the hell was on that note?

I finally switched off the computer and headed to bed, where I tossed and turned until I heard the sound of the front door being unlocked when Tiffany arrived home. She came into our bedroom and was tiptoeing around until I let her know that it was unnecessary.

She came over to the bed, sat down, and kissed me on the lips.

"How'd it go tonight?" she asked.

"Not well," I said. "I can't find any skeletons in this guy's closet. Nothing that would cause him to take the big dive."

"So what are you going to do?"

"I'm going to find religion," I said wryly. "At the God's Way Church."

She leaned over to me and whispered in my ear, "Not yet." She cooed, "Not until we go, toe-to-toe."

And so we did.

SEVEN

I arrived forty minutes early to attend the regularly-scheduled nine o'clock Sunday services at the God's Way Church and I was glad that I had. The funeral for Pastor Roy had been put off until the following weekend, but the crowd of people attending the service today seemed extraordinary. I circled the parking lot several times before finally lucking out and getting what appeared to be one of the few remaining spots.

Over the past several days, the media had a field day with the tragic story. By now Roy Mentzer had been identified and the next of kin were notified, so it was fair game. The local paper had led the charge by doing several front-page articles on the death of this beloved man and local legend. The articles typically got several of the facts incorrect - which was par for the course for our daily fish-wrapper - and tended to go into great detail about the story of Pastor Roy's inspiring life.

The topic of whether it was a suicide or not was handled gingerly, but always with a hint of something darker; they had to sell papers after all. The fact that there was no suicide note left behind put everything into question, and this allowed speculation to run rampant. The paper always covered their posterior by referred to the incident as "a mysterious crash," and said that the authorities were "vigorously investigating." The police were no doubt looking into the same elements of Roy and his family's life as I had, and probably were coming up empty as well.

Along with expressing shock and asking for everyone's prayers, the church's second in command, Pastor Jim Harkin, was quoted several times as saying that the crash must have been the result of "an unfortunate accident," or "mechanical failure." He was adamant that it wasn't suicide, as many - in and out of the press - had speculated. He said there was no reason why the beloved Pastor Roy would do such a thing. Harkin promised to push for a thorough investigation, and to bring in the NTSB if necessary to determine the root cause.

Although I knew otherwise by witnessing the event firsthand, I had to agree with Harkin's assessment; if there was a wolf, or the Grim Reaper, knocking on Roy Mentzer's door, I couldn't spot him either.

I got out of my car and took a good look around before entering the main building. Several news vans were parked on the street off the lot and had their satellite antennas deployed and beaming back to the station. Cameramen trailed reporters who were on the hunt to get juicy sound bites from the stunned congregation. For the most part, no one was playing ball, and church members were waving off requests for interviews. Near the entrance to the main church, people were milling about in small groups and talking quietly, some leaning forward conspiratorially.

"It's terrible isn't it? Just terrible!"

I turned toward the sound and saw a woman hobbling toward me in the parking lot. In reality, she wasn't necessarily heading at me, but toward the entrance, and I just happened to be in her path.

She was in her mid to late fifties, of average height and weight, and had a mass of tangled blond-brown hair that looked as if it had been coifed with an eggbeater in a windstorm. She wore no makeup, and was dressed in a dark-blue dress that had a hem in need of repair. Over the dress, she wore a powder blue sweater that had a stain on one sleeve, and was worn threadbare at each of the elbows. There were flakes of dandruff on her shoulders, and her panty hose had a run on her left shin. She teetered in high heels like a child playing dress up in Mommy's clothes.

"Yes it is," I said somberly, not knowing whether she was referring specifically to Pastor Roy's demise, or the untoward attention from the media.

"All of them!" she exclaimed, as she caught up to me, gesturing wildly to the news vans. "All they want is dirt. First Pastor Roy…then, the media."

She leaned closer then and spat out, "They're The Devil you know; the liberal media."

Besides her wild hair and poor grooming, she had a habit of blinking her eyes as she spoke. It was as if her mouth and peepers were somehow linked and she was simulcasting her words in semaphore.

"I know," I said, proffering a hand. "Jack Swanson."

She shifted a well-worn leather-bound bible from her right hand to her left, and we shook. "Beverly Tate."

I shook her hand. It was ice cold and sweaty.

We started walking toward the entrance together and she ran her free hand through her tangled hair. Several more bits of dandruff drifted down onto her shoulders like Lilliputian snowflakes.

"How long have you been coming here?" I asked.

"Sixteen and a half years," she answered, her eyelids fluttering. Then her tone changed, and she stopped abruptly in her tracks.

"Wait a minute," she said suspiciously. "You aren't with the media, are you?"

"No, I'm not."

She studied me warily, eyes narrowing.

"Well I know everyone here, and I've never seen you before."

"It's because I've never been here before," I said as easily as if it was the honest to God truth - which, thanks to our proximity to The Almighty's house where he might just send a lightning bolt my way for fibbing, it was. "I read about Pastor Roy and all of his good work in the paper, and I thought that maybe his death was a sign that I should do something more with my life. That's all."

She stood studying me, not saying a word, and waiting for me to blink, shift my gaze, or for my nose to grow. After a few moments, I said, "I guess I'll see you inside then Beverly."

I turned toward the entrance and continued walking toward it.

“Wait a minute,” she called out from behind me.

I turned to see her tottering up to me in her shoes. How she didn’t break an ankle was a miracle.

“It’s just…well you know, a girl can’t be too careful is all.”

I had no idea what she meant by that statement, but I agreed with her.

We reached the entrance to the main building and that’s when Beverly’s verbal floodgates really broke loose. She did, in fact, seem to know everybody. And she had something to say to everyone we encountered. If she was animated with her gestures before, now they were running at full tilt. Every interception with another church member triggered a rapid-fire oral outburst. It was like her head was a blender overflowing with opinions, comments, and critiques - and it was switched onto high. While she was busy yammering, I took the opportunity to look around the interior.

The campus of the God’s Way Church comprised one main building, with several outer, or satellite, buildings. Inside the main building was a large reception area with doors leading off to other rooms. Several groups of people were milling around or engaged in conversation. Ushers were doing a land office business directing people to the proper venues. Three sets of large double doors led to the main auditorium, which was directly in front of us. From my vantage point I could tell, without even stepping into it, that it must have been capacious.

Several other doors and hallways led off to other rooms, and I spied signs with arrows that read: Children’s Ministry, Café, and Bookstore. I took a quick glance at Beverly, and seeing that she was fully engrossed in an animated conversation with an older gentleman, decided to extend my tour a bit. I was sure I'd encounter Beverly again. She didn't strike me as someone you could shake very easily.

I sauntered over to the Café and stepped inside. It was a modest setup with about a dozen tables, most of which were occupied by patrons. I noticed several of the customers were wearing AA sobriety pins. A long glass case was setup at one end of the eatery and displayed offerings of cold sandwiches, donuts, and other pastries. The line was three deep at the register, and a coffee with a bagel and creamed cheese seemed to be the hot ticket. The only remarkable thing about the Café was the fact that it had several large flat-screen TVs mounted high up on the wall that displayed what appeared to be the stage from the interior of the main sanctuary. Several musicians tuning up instruments were visible on the screen, but there was no audio.

I exited the café and walked a few steps over to the God's Way bookstore. It was about the size of your average airport gift shop, but it wasn't doing near as brisk a business as the Café. A few people were strolling the aisles between tall shelves filled with bibles, greeting cards, crosses, and every type of inspirational refrigerator magnet you could imagine, but the cash register wasn't singing. More noteworthy than the merchandise, was the fact that convex anti-shoplifting mirrors were affixed to the walls in the corners along with security cameras. I guess even God didn't hold with inventory shrinkage.

After a quick pass of the bookstore, I left and stepped back into the main reception area. I saw the sign pointing to children's ministry but thinking it might draw too much attention that a stranger would be roaming around in there, I decided to pass on it.

As I moved back through the reception area toward the main auditorium, I tried to eavesdrop on snippets of conversation from the groups of people that I passed by. They were mostly speaking in low tones, but I have excellent hearing and caught some bits and pieces.

"...just so, so sad..."

"...his family must feel..."

"...bigger plans for him in heaven..."

"...God's will..."

"...testing their faith..."

But then there were also these:

"...so then, what do you think really..."

"...what's going to happen now..."

"...Pastor Harkin, I guess..."

I stepped into the main hall of the God's Way Church and it was every bit as expansive as I had expected. And it was completely different from any of my previous - and painful - experiences with houses of worship.

As religious categories go, I could best be described as a recovering Catholic. I was an only child, and my father had been a career military man. It was not a great family situation to begin with, and I spent nearly all of my youth being schlepped around from one army base to another. The difficulties with growing up in this fashion were further exacerbated by the fact that my father and mother were also devout Catholics. Most bases didn't have parochial schools, and so on top of being constantly on the move and never having time to build any long-lasting friendships, I attended Catholic school off base, further isolating me from the other kids. I hated every minute of it and I couldn't wait until I was old enough to tell the priests, the nuns, and the Pope that I was moving on. My mother predeceased my dad, and when my father died years later, I attended his funeral at the church and vowed that it would be the last time I ever stepped foot into one. I had kept that promise until today.

In stark contrast to the ornate but cold gaudiness of most Catholic churches, the main chamber of God's Way was more like a modern college auditorium than anything else. The floors were carpeted in deep blue, and the chairs were nicely padded and arraigned in a shallow arc that faced the main stage. The stage itself was at least the length and depth of a basketball court, and it was well illuminated by racks of stage lights and floods mounted high above. A giant cross was attached to the wall at center stage. A large God's Way sign flanked one side of the cross, and a large styrofoam dove in flight was affixed on the other side.

On the stage were at least a dozen and a half musicians with their instruments: guitar, bass, keyboard, harp, cello, drums, woodwind, and brass, all busy and getting ready to perform. Several huge monitors mounted over the stage displayed the action in real time, and the video and audio were recorded and mixed from a giant camera and soundboard that was manned by two engineers in the back of the room.

The seats were starting to fill up, so I decided to grab one while there were some still available. I turned and began walking toward a place in the back right corner, but before I could take two steps, Beverly was upon me, making as much noise in her clod-hoppers as a Clydesdale with a loose shoe.

"Oh there you are," she exclaimed, her eyes fluttering with every word. "I thought maybe you had gotten cold feet."

"No. Never."

"Good. Let me show you the best seats. We'd better hurry."

Before I could respond or protest, she grabbed me by the arm and dragged me back to the center aisle, and to a row of seats only five away from the stage.

"The best," she promised.

We sat down and before long the seats around us began to fill up. At nine o'clock on the dot, the band launched into their first set. Several vocalists joined in, and pretty soon the overhead displays changed from a live shot of the stage to scenes of beautiful beach sunsets, mountains, and lush spring meadows. Superimposed on top of the images were the words to the songs, all of which were meant to inspire and glorify The Almighty.

Pretty soon, musicians who could free one or both arms had them outstretched and were reaching for the heavens. Several in the congregation were soon on their feet and followed suit. It was good music, and I'd have to admit, I found my foot tapping to the beat through several songs.

In the meantime, I noticed that the late Pastor Roy's family had entered from a side door and were escorted to seats in the front row, near the center. They strained to put on brave faces, but understandably, they were still in shock. Roy's daughter Christina had a pronounced redness in her eyes, and his widow,

Betty, looked especially worn. Together, the family sat mutely through several more songs, not singing, standing, or raising their arms.

Finally, Pastor Jim Harkin took the stage. The overhead displays cut to a close-up of him standing at the podium. He was a good-looking man in his sixties, and had a nice head of thick gray hair. His face was very tan, and I could imagine him as no stranger to the golf course or tennis courts.

He looked briefly in the direction of Roy's grieving family, and nodded sympathetically to them, before turning back to the congregation.

"This is, understandably, a very difficult time for all of us," he began somberly. "And one that will try all our wills, and that reaches all the way to the very core of our faith."

He paused to let the words sink in, and I sensed several people in the crowd nodding their heads in agreement.

"But we are not alone in our struggle," Harkin reassured the crowd. "Matthew 5:4 tells us that, 'Blessed are those who mourn, for they will be comforted.'"

As he spoke, the overhead screens changed to a blank background with the words of the scripture superimposed on them. Several people in the audience opened their bibles and turned to the passage.

"And Romans 8:18 tells us, 'I consider that our present sufferings are not worth comparing with the glory that will be revealed in us.'"

Harkin paused briefly, and then quickly changed gears.

"My brothers and sisters in faith, adding to our terrible grief, is the fact that some have tried to say that this was an intentional act on the part of Pastor Roy."

Harkin looked about at the stone faces in the crowd and then swept an arm toward the rear of the room.

"And some of these same misguided voices," he said sternly. "Are at this very moment parked right outside our house of God."

Beverly took the opportunity to tug on my arm. "See what I told you about the media?" she hissed in her stage whisper. " The Devil!"

"God and I can assure you, my brothers and sisters," Harkin continued. "That this was not the case. Pastor Roy, for all of his tireless efforts, still had plenty of our Lord's work to do on this earth - and he would *not* leave us unattended!"

Without turning my head around, I stole a glance at some of the faces in the packed house. Some of the congregates were nodding emphatically in agreement, some sat stone faced, either from shock, or quite possibly, from having their own opinions on the matter.

Harkin continued to preach and make his case that it had been an unfortunate accident, a mechanical failure. He also sought to reassure the crowd that Pastor Roy was now serving God in a higher capacity, and that The Almighty had big plans for him.

After about twenty minutes, Harkin concluded his sermon and stepped off to the side. He approached the Mentzer family and comforted each one individually with a hug or by laying his hands on them.

While Harkin was busy with the Mentzer clan, the band struck up again, and was filling the giant chamber with uplifting tunes. The opportunity was not wasted by the financial arm of God's Way and pretty soon, men with velour-lined baskets began passing them from one end of a row to another. Many in the congregation made their offerings in small tithing envelopes, but some dropped in currency, and I even heard the occasional jingle of coins as they passed from man's hand to God's purse.

When the basket reached me I dropped in a fifty-dollar bill and I noticed that it caused Beverly's eyes to widen some. If she had any lingering doubt about me being with the news media, it dissipated along with my generous donation.

At a certain point, people began to get up from their seats and head out into the reception area. Beverly and I followed suit, and I began to think that my spiritual commitment was over for the day. I was soon to learn that it was far from complete.

"I usually get a coffee now," Beverly said, as we made our way through the reception area and into the café, which was doing an even brisker business. There were two large industrial percolators, one each of regular and decaffeinated coffee, off to the side of the main counter and we headed toward them.

"If you just want regular coffee and don't care about all that fancy latte stuff, this is where you go," she explained.

She grabbed a styrofoam cup of regular coffee and added six sugars and two creamers to it. I grabbed a cup of black joe and we moved off to the side. We had only been stationary for a few seconds before she spotted someone she had to introduce me to.

"Edie, this is Jack Swanson," she said rapidly, to a matronly woman in a dark-green dress that was two sizes too small for her. "He's new to our ministry, and I'm going to show him around."

She spun around to me suddenly, her sacchariferous coffee sloshing out of the cup and onto the floor. She didn't even notice.

"You are going to go to our bible study class, aren't you, Jack?" she asked.

"Well I wasn't planning on it, and I don't have a bible I'm afraid."

She quickly grabbed me by the arm, abandoning Edie on the spot, and towed me into gift shop.

"They have all kinds in here if you want to get one now, or they have loaners in bible study."

"Are you going to bible study?" I asked, already knowing the answer.

"Of course!" she said incredulously.

I considered the situation and thought that it might be good to attend the study class to gather some more intel, so I agreed to go and let Beverly pick my bible.

After examining several versions, she decided that a King James version would be a good "starter" one for me to have, and so we paid for it and headed to the bible study classroom. For the next hour and a half, Beverly and myself, along with approximately forty other eager souls, read, dissected, and analyzed various scripture. I found myself hopelessly lost and requiring constant instruction as to where to find the designated passage. With Beverly's help I got through it, although the hour and a half didn't exactly bear the fruit I had hoped for. For the most part, people were too busy discussing the verses to waste time gossiping. I realized I'd have to find a better forum in which to mine dirt, and wondered wryly if you could return a bible with low mileage on it.

After the class, we made our way out to the God's Way parking lot, which had emptied out considerably. I walked Beverly to her car. She began telling me all about the church: who was who, how she volunteered as a secretary on Tuesdays and every other Thursday, how it was all so terrible, Pastor Roy's poor family, how this would test everyone's faith, how the Lord guides us, and how we would all get through it…

As she delivered her seemingly endless soliloquy, she clutched a ring of keys in her hand, and they clanged and jangled with every word she spoke. I had to admit the woman was a fountain of knowledge about the church, but she was wearing on my nerves.

Just as Beverly was in the midst of reciting her own philosophy of faith to me, I caught a flash of movement out of the corner of my eye, a familiarly-hued movement. I turned just in time to see a cream-colored 2016 Mercedes-Benz coupe, with no plates, as it squealed out of the God's Way parking lot.

EIGHT

"So you couldn't catch her?" Tiffany asked me.

"No," I said. "This woman, Beverly - who is next to impossible to get away from - was standing right next to me. The Mercedes could have been in another time zone by the time I was able to break away and pick up the pursuit."

After finally shaking off Beverly, I had come straight home from the God's Way Church. Tiffany and I were seated in a pair of matching Adirondack chairs on the upper deck of the three-story house that we owned on The Strand in pricey Manhattan Beach. Between us, we had a bowl of ceviche and some blue corn chips. A pitcher of Margaritas and two glasses with salt on the rims rounded out the banquet. Our chairs faced out toward the gorgeous Pacific Ocean.

We had purchased the house jointly, soon after we recovered a cache of rare gems that Russian mobster, Viktor Durov, had paid to Tiffany's late husband for performing identity-altering surgery on him. The gems were stolen and extremely valuable, but they also had been inscribed with a laser to prevent them from being sold on the open market.

It took a while, but I finally found a crooked gemologist/cutter who would re-cut the registered stones. He wasn't happy about doing it, but he was even less happy that I would follow through on my threat to spill the beans on him about certifying hundreds of thousands of dollars of "blood" diamonds as "conflict-free." Our newly re-cut gems had diminished in value, but not enough that Tiffany and I couldn't have our own magnificent piece of the American Dream.

"And you're not even sure that it was Red, right Jack?" Tiffany asked.

"No. By the time I saw the car, I only caught a glance of it from the rear; I couldn't see enough detail through the back window to be sure one way or the other."

"But your gut tells you it was her?'

"Yeah. I don't know why, but it does."

"So what now?" Tiffany asked. "Do you think you can find her?"

I took a swallow of Margarita and stared out to the sea, pondering my options. A neophyte on a stand-up paddleboard caught a small wave and rode it only for a few feet before pearling the nose and wiping out. But it was such a gorgeous day; even he was having fun.

I knew that I could try to see if God's Way had security cameras in the parking lot that might have picked up Red going to her car. I didn't see any cameras inside or outside the building, other than in the gift shop, but I wasn't looking for them either. And even if the church had cameras, getting access to the tapes would probably require a huge amount of subterfuge. Even if I was successful, all it might prove was that she was there. Without getting to the paper registration, I still wouldn't have a name to go with the face.

I could also stake out the parking lot in the hopes that Red would come back. But she might not, and then I would have burned up a bunch of time for nothing.

Or I could try pumping Beverly for some information, but that might re-trigger her paranoia that I was with the liberal media. She would brand me a veritable wolf in sheep's clothing, and would clam up on me. As much effort as she was, I needed to keep her as a possible source of information on the church and its members.

Without answering Tiffany's question, I turned the tables, and asked her one of my own.

"If it was her," I wondered out loud. "Why do you think she came to the church?"

Now it was Tiffany's turn to ponder, but she couldn't do that on an empty stomach, so she dipped a tortilla chip into the marinated seafood mixture. I followed her by filling my own palate. We both washed it down with another sip of our "maggies."

"Well," Tiffany began. "If it *was* her, it definitely wasn't a coincidence."

"Exactly," I said. "The story's all over the news. She'd have to have been in a coma to not know about the crash."

Tiffany nodded, then wiped some of the Margarita salt away from her mouth. She was deep in thought and I didn't disturb her. Finally, she turned to me.

"I don't know, Jack. Do you think she would be so sick as to want to go to the church to see all of the heartache she had caused, kind of like a perverse thrill?"

"You mean like an arsonist watching the fire he had started - just for the excitement of it?" I offered.

"Yes."

"Maybe." I shrugged. "And if she does indeed tick that way, then she'll be sure to be there for the big one."

"The big one?"

"Pastor Roy's funeral," I said. "It's next Saturday."

NINE

With not much to do except wait until Roy Mentzer's funeral, I busied myself during the week with getting back to my regular work. Blackmailing is in many ways, no different than any other business. I had accounts payables to take care of for such things as re-mailing services, P.O. boxes, and surveillance equipment. As well as accounts receivables to keep track of. These were the payments from my marks, some of which needed gentle nudges to keep them current with their obligations.

On top of this donkey work, I was busy getting ready to lean on a medical marijuana dispensary in Venice that had in its employ a "doctor" who was operating under a revoked license. The old sawbones had no problem prescribing high-potency cannabis as the cure-all for everything from colorectal cancer to bunions, and as a result, the dispensary made tons of money. All of their income was in cash, thanks to federal money-laundering regulations that prohibited banks from enabling ATM or credit card transactions.

When everything was in place, and I had the irrefutable evidence on the doctor, I knew my payday was going to be as tasty as a well-rolled "fattie."

The media coverage of Pastor Roy and God's Way had disappeared from the radar screen for a few days, only to reappear when the police released their final report about the incident. The headline in the local paper stated what most in the media, and possibly a few from the God's Way flock, had suspected: Their beloved shepherd's death was a suicide.

The vehicle had been recovered, impounded, and examined by a team of forensic specialists from the NTSB and the insurance company. Together, they determined that prior to the crash, there had been no mechanical issues with the car's steering, power plant, or braking systems. The findings, coupled with the statements by the two eyewitnesses that the car had accelerated toward the cliff after it turned onto the dirt lot and the fact that Roy's seat belt was unhooked, pretty much sealed the deal. No mention was made of the investigators finding the note that I had seen Pastor Roy leaving the motel with, but it probably got swept away with the waves and was at the bottom of the Pacific.

A short statement from Pastor Jim Harkin simply said, "God's Way Church does not agree with the findings, and we still believe it was an unfortunate accident." Other church members, requesting anonymity, admitted that although it was hard to accept, they didn't refute the investigation's findings.

* * *

I arrived extra early at the God's Way Church on Saturday morning and parked at a far corner of the lot near a donut shop. The parking space was slightly elevated and offered me a view of not just the outside lot, but of the entrance to the God's Way parking structure as well.

A veteran of many stakeouts, I knew from painful experience just how arduous they could be, and what to bring along to make life easier. To this end, I brought a couple of sandwiches, a thermos of coffee, some bottled water, an empty juice bottle with a wide mouth to relieve myself in, and some aspirin.

Also, if the opportunity didn't present itself to directly brace Red, I had a backup plan to cover my bases. Besides getting a look at her paper registration to trace it, I also brought a GPS tracking device that I planned to conceal on her car in the off chance it was registered to someone else.

I also had a plan to videotape the parking lot should I have to leave my vehicle for some reason. Not wanting to draw attention, I didn't use my standard tripod mounted video camera to capture the events. Instead I had a dash cam that I had stealthily tucked into a box of tissue sitting on top of the dashboard. The camera was Bluetooth enabled so no external wires were needed, and it synched to a DVR mounted under the seat that could record uninterrupted for over twenty hours. The hard drive unit was Wi-Fi enabled, and would broadcast a real time stream to my phone, should I need to view it remotely.

I switched on the camera and double-checked to make sure it was recording onto the drive. Then I pulled out my phone and checked the live stream. It looked great. Now all I had to do was wait for Red to arrive. Maybe that would be in a half-hour, an hour, two hours, or until I died a crazed, feeble old man.

It took about forty minutes for the first cars to arrive at God's Way. A large, full-sized van with no windows pulled up and several young bucks got out. They reminded me of some of the musicians I had seen last week. When they opened the van doors and began wheeling instruments and amplifiers into Gods Way, I was vindicated.

Pretty soon, more cars began pulling in and then more still. Some of the occupants were also musicians, but others appeared to be either church members or staff.

At about eight-fifteen, several local TV news vans pulled up as well and deployed their booms. In a short time, the cameramen and the reporters climbed out, and began running sound and video checks, as well as hunting for vulnerable prey.

Since the story had broken about Roy's suicide, the media attention had rekindled itself from a few glowing embers to, if not a bonfire, at least a good conflagration. The TV crews no doubt wanted to capitalize on the raw emotions of the moment, and I'm sure they were hoping to get at least one or two good sobbing breakdowns on camera for the evening news.

"Hey, what are you doing in there?"

I jumped instinctively and turned toward the sound. It was Beverly Tate, standing just outside my driver's side window.

She had approached undetected from my left side, the area of my peripheral vision that no longer existed. Like any one of the other senses, people take their binocular vision for granted - until they no longer have it.

Recovering after the loss of my left eye, I was amazed at the difficulty of functioning at the level of normalcy I was used to. Besides embarrassing moments like this one, where people walk up and startle you, you also find yourself inadvertently bumping into people as you walk, and with your depth perception all but gone, you knock over things when you reach for them. I don't know how many spills I cleaned up in the beginning just trying to go about my daily life.

I switched on the ignition and hit the button to lower the window.

"Waiting for you," I smiled. "I was hoping we could sit together again."

This elicited a crooked smile and a faint blush on Beverly's face.

She was dressed in a simple black shift with a scoop neck and long sleeves. Other than highlighting her chronic dandruff problem, the dress probably would have worked well for the occasion had Beverly not tried her hand at accessorizing it with a powder blue belt cinched around her waist, and a pair of bright red shoes. Her panty hose were intact with no runs this time out, but her red shoes were scuffed at the toes.

Eyes blinking rapidly in time to her words, she said, "Well let's hurry up! All of the good seats will be taken pretty soon."

I didn't really want to head into the service until I had made sure that every car had arrived, but I was busted now. And if I remained sitting here it would draw too much suspicion from old wobbles. I raised the window back up and grabbed my coat jacket. I was just about to close the door when Beverly stopped me.

"Wait a minute," she said. "Don't forget your bible."

I reached back into the car, grabbed my holy book and closed the door.

As soon as I had cleared the vehicle, she unexpectedly gave me a big hug, burying the side of her face into my chest.

"I'm glad you came," she sputtered. "It will make it easier."

"For me too," I said.

I broke away and pulled on my coat.

"You look nice!" Beverly said.

"You too," I lied.

We walked together toward the church and I took one final look at the parking lot before we entered. By now, cars trying to get in were backed up onto the street and causing traffic snarls. I looked, but didn't see Red's Mercedes-Benz anywhere in the crush. Oh well, at least the camera was still rolling. I could always try to break away from Beverly and fast-forward through the footage on my phone in the bathroom. And if Red showed her pretty face, I could try to get to her before she left.

We entered the front reception area and not surprisingly, it hadn't changed physically, but the mood of the place certainly had. The atmosphere was much more somber, and the few people who were conversing, were speaking in quiet tones. How much this had to do with the report that it was a suicide was anyone's guess. Even Beverly was subdued. She still had to say something to everyone she saw, but her comments were limited to simple greetings and gentle words of encouragement.

Entering the main chamber, Beverly and I saw that the seats we had occupied the previous week were taken, so she steered us toward others that she guaranteed were just as good. At floor level, in front of the seats, and centered in the cavernous hall, was a brushed-silver metal casket resting on an aluminum extension trolley. The casket was closed and several sprays of flowers on stands were arraigned around it, along with a wood-framed portrait of Pastor Roy. The picture chosen for the portrait wasn't the stock photo from the God's Way website, and it looked as if had been rendered from a favorite family photo. The resolution was less than desirable, but the picture showed a beaming Roy Mentzer, looking as if he had everything in the world to live for.

"Oh my," Beverly breathed frightfully when she spied the casket and the flowers. She clutched my arm tightly in her hands and I attempted to steady her - which was more difficult than with most people.

I could be sympathetic to her emotions though. Seeing a casket, and knowing that a loved one was ensconced in it for the rest of eternity, puts a sense of finality on the whole affair.

We made it to our seats without incident, and while the band tuned up, I noticed Jim Harkin and several of the church's other ministers and elders milling about at the front of the auditorium. They were talking in low tones and wore, if not stern, at least serious expressions.

After a moment, one of them turned toward the main entrance as something got his attention. It must have been important, because he whispered something to the others and soon, they were all walking toward the back of the room.

I turned in my seat and saw the group of them greeting another man and woman at the rear. Handshakes and hugs were exchanged all around. Beverly caught me watching all of the action from my chair, and began a play by play.

"That's Pastor Ben Howard and his wife, Sheila. They're from the New Light Church over in Carson."

"Hmmm. Are there other pastors from other churches here to pay their respects?" I asked.

"Oh yes!" Beverly brightened, as if it were a real soiree. She began pointing excitedly around the room, her arm nearly clipping me in the head. "There's Pastor John from His Spirit Church in Torrance, and Pastor Ed from First Faith in Redondo Beach, and Pastor Steve from..."

She said it all so fast in her machine gun oratory I could have never remembered a single name if my life depended on it. Then all of a sudden, she stopped in mid-sentence, her eyes narrowing and her mood darkening noticeably. Something had stolen her attention near the entrance to the main ministry.

I turned toward the object of her interest and saw a tall, good-looking man in a dark suit striding confidently into the hall. He was in his fifties, and trailing him was an attractive woman with shoulder length blond hair whom I guessed to be his wife.

As with the other visiting men of the cloth and their wives, salutations, hugs, and air-kisses were offered. But I thought I noticed a distinct coolness between this new couple and some of the God's Way clergy.

I turned toward Beverly and jerked my head in the new man's direction. "Who is that?" I asked.

Beverly turned toward me, her eyes on fire and her mouth twisted up in a snarl. "That's Pastor Ronald Sommers. He's from Pathways' Christian fellowship."

She leaned closer to me so that our faces were almost touching.

"And he's trying to steal our church!"

TEN

The final service for Pastor Roy lasted over two hours. There were more musical breakouts than usual, more sermons, and along with a slide show, a lengthy eulogy of Roy Mentzer's inspiring life by Pastor Harkin. At one point during the service, Betty Mentzer took the podium, and with her children at her side, delivered an emotional tribute to her late husband and his work. Sniffles and outright bawling was occasionally heard from the packed crowd, and I doubted if there were many dry eyes in the house. At one point, Beverly broke down next to me and buried her face in my chest. I put my arm around her and held her tightly until she recovered. Several of the congregates also stood up and shared memories about their own interactions with Pastor Roy throughout the years. Many of them struggled against their emotions to finish their stories. The visiting ministers, and most importantly, Sommers and his wife, took reserved spots in the front row alongside the Mentzer family.

At the conclusion there was an announcement that the funeral procession would be departing from the main parking lot in thirty minutes, and that everyone should follow the police escorts.

Realizing that the bathrooms would be crowded, and trying to take advantage of the situation, people rushed out of the auditorium and charged into them. Beverly, slowed by her clumsy gait, wasn't able to make tracks in time and was stuck in a line of women that stretched ten feet out the door. I took the opportunity to relieve myself as well and headed to the men's room to find a notable, albeit smaller, queue.

While I was waiting my turn, I pulled out my phone and fast-forwarded through the video that had been captured of the parking lot by my secret dash cam. The line in the men's room moved rapidly, and I was only able to scroll through the footage one time before it was my turn at the stalls.

I stepped back out into the main reception area and saw that Beverly had yet to cross the threshold to the women's facilities. Figuring it might be wise to get her alone to glean more info about what she meant with her "stealing our church" comment, I went up to her and asked, "Did you want to ride with me to the funeral Beverly? It might help to cut down on the traffic congestion."

She smiled and her eyes blinked uncontrollably as if I had just asked her to the senior prom.

"Oh y…y…yes!" she stammered.

I nodded and moved away from the door, hoping she wouldn't pee herself with excitement before she made it into the stall. In the meantime, I went through the video footage once again. And, once again, I came to the same conclusion: Red was nowhere to be found.

By the time Beverly and I exited the church, a black hearse carrying Pastor Roy's casket was already sitting at exit of the parking lot. The hearse was followed by a stretch limo, and several cars had already queued up behind it. We climbed into my van, and before I did anything else, I removed the box of tissue with the camera in it from the dashboard and set it behind us.

"Can't drive with anything that obscures your view," I explained.

I waited until we fell into line with other cars in the funeral procession before I broached the subject of Pastor Sommers with Beverly.

"So what did you mean back there about Pastor Sommers wanting to steal the church?" I asked casually.

"Well," she said. "I guess maybe 'steal' is kind of strong language. He wants God's Way to merge with his church, and to become part of their family."

"Family?"

"Oh yes." Beverly explained, "Sometimes churches will merge with others in order to become larger and be able to do more of The Lord's work. It's something called dynergy or tynergy I think."

"You mean, synergy?" I offered.

"Yes, that's it."

"And Sommers wants God's Way to merge with his church. What did you call it; Pathways?"

"Pathways' Christian fellowship. And yes, he wants us to merge with him."

"How do you know this?" I asked easily, acting as if it really didn't matter to me.

"Well," she began. "I volunteer in the office on Tuesdays, and every other Thursday you know, and sometimes - well sometimes, you just can't help but hear the scuttlebutt."

At the utterance of the word from her own lips, she immediately stiffened and put her hand to her mouth. "Oops, I'm sorry," she apologized. "Is scuttlebutt a curse word?"

"No, I don't think so," I assured her.

Relieved, she continued on. By now, the hearse had reached the entrance to the cemetery and traffic had started to backup. Beverly and I were so far back in the procession, I guessed I still had another good couple of minutes to get her to spill the beans about the behind the scenes situation at God's Way Church.

"And so anyway, the pastors always have a leadership meeting on Thursdays, and I happened to be in the other room doing filing when I heard them yelling. Well, they weren't yelling - not exactly, but their voices were raised. You know what I mean don't you?"

"Of course."

"I heard some of them saying that it was the only way we were going to survive, but others were arguing against it."

"So who decides?" I asked.

"Well," Beverly said. "I don't know that much about it, but I know that they all vote. But Pastor Harkin is now in charge, and so that means that he has majority voting rights."

"Could he overrule them?" I asked.

Beverly considered the question for a moment, her head cocked and her eyes rolled upward as if The Lord himself was going to write the answer on the face of a cloud. In the bright sunlight of the car, I could see her dandruff flakes, sparkling like tiny gems on the shoulders of her dark dress.

"I'm not sure," she admitted, turning back to look at me. "I think he has to have at least some of the others to go his way."

"And what is his way?" I asked.

"Oh, he's all for it, " Beverly said. "He's the one saying it's a matter of survival."

* * *

At the internment of Pastor Roy Mentzer, there were still more speeches, and plenty more final tears. Betty Mentzer and her children sat stoically in the front row in folding chairs that had been setup under a large white canopy on the grass. Behind them were others whom I assumed to be close family, and then further back, the visiting clergy from the other churches in the area. I attempted to watch carefully for any sort of dynamic - good or bad - between Harkin and Sommers, but they each sat in their respective seats and stared straight ahead.

After the ceremony had concluded, and everyone had paid their final respects, I returned with Beverly to the God's Way parking lot. I didn't think it appropriate to continue our conversation regarding the proposed church merger and the infighting it had spawned, and so we drove in silence the few miles of the return trip.

I parked the van and walked Beverly to her car, wondering all the time if she was expecting me to kiss her or to ask for her phone number. I didn't give her the chance though, and took control of the situation by hugging her before she had an opportunity to offer me either her mouth or her number. I couldn't tell if she was disappointed or thrilled, and so I bid her good-bye and headed back to the van, my mind whirling with the newfound knowledge of a possible palace coup at God's Way Church, and how I could learn more about it.

* * *

Realizing that Beverly Tate might have spies in the office who might report back to her that I had gone to see Harkin, I decided to meet with him discreetly off-site. After getting through to him on the phone, I introduced myself as Steve Lane, and told him that I was very interested in setting up a foundation within God's Way Church, but that I was a very private person and wanted to remain anonymous. He assured me that he understood completely, and we agreed to meet for lunch at The Kettle Restaurant in Manhattan Beach. He was waiting expectantly for me at a booth in a corner of the restaurant when I arrived. I extended my hand and he rose.

"Pastor Harkin?"

"Yes," he said pumping my hand. "Mister Lane."

I could tell that he was already looking at me and noticing my eye-patch, trying to place me. He may have seen me and recognized me from my two prior visits to God's Way or he may not have. After all, it had been a crazy couple of weeks, and there were thousands of members in the room. Whether he remembered me or not, he didn't let on.

I sat down and noted that there were two menus already lying on the table. Not wanting to be interrupted by the waitress at an inopportune time, I picked one up and started scanning it. Harkin followed suit, and together we sat silently making our selections. In a moment, our server came by and took our order. When she left, Harkin looked up to me.

"First of all," he said. "You have my word that your anonymity will remain protected. Many of our donors feel the same way, and this conversation will go no farther than this table."

"I'm glad to hear that Pastor Harkin, because I don't think you'll want this conversation to leave the table either."

He looked at me oddly for a second, the features of his tanned face twisted up in puzzlement.

"I'm afraid I don't under -" he began before I cut him off.

"My name's not Lane," I said. "And I'm not here to setup a foundation. I'll get right to point. Why are you so hell bent to sell out God's Way to Sommers' church?"

"What is this?" he said indignantly. "Why did you drag me here on false pretenses? That is none of your business!"

" I think it is," I retorted.

"And why is that?" Harkin shot back, his voice rising slightly.

I set a flash drive on the table in front of him and gestured to it.

"Because I have video that shows what drove Pastor Roy to commit suicide."

Harkin took a deep intake of air, alternately staring at me and then at the flash drive. He picked it up and held it in his hand, turning it over and staring at it for a long time. Finally, he set it back down gently and looked up at me.

"Well then," he said flatly. "I guess that makes two of us."

ELEVEN

I sat there stunned. It was if the entire world had ground to screeching halt around me. I don't know if my jaw had dropped, but I wouldn't have been surprised to learn that it had. If I thought I was going to rock Harkin's world by dropping the bombshell on him about the video, now it was his chance to turn the tables on me.

"What, what are you talking about?" I stammered.

"Oh no, not so fast." Harkin shot back. "First of all; who are you, and where did you get your video?"

"You can call me Jack, just Jack."

"Okay Jack," Harkin said with a bit of sneer. "And why do you just happen to have a video of Pastor Roy?"

"Because that's what I do for a living," I said. "I get damming info on people and then I sell it back to them to keep it quiet. Mentzer just happened to be the guy in the crosshairs this time around."

The waitress arrived with our food and we both fell quiet. I started to pick up my fork, but then I noticed that Harkin had begun to silently pray over his meal. I waited until he was done and had picked up his utensils before continuing. We each sat silently, picking at our food, as well as trying to digest what the other man had said.

After pushing his food around his plate for a few moments, Harkin broke the silence.

"Okay," he said smugly. "I think I've got the picture about you Jack - or whatever you say your name is. And what you do for a living."

Then he paused, and added for emphasis, "And I hope you sleep good at night."

Sorry Pastor, I thought wryly. *After a decade of squeezing people for their failings, don't you think I've heard that dig a million times before?*

"Oh no you don't," I fired back. "You hope I'm tortured like I'm in Hades already, burning in hellfire on a spit. Just to let you know, Harkin, I sleep like a baby at night. And you know why I do? Because I'm not the one cheating on my spouse. How long had the good pastor and his wife been married, twelve years? And then Betty has a hysterectomy in 2009, at the tender age of thirty-eight? That's a tough thing for any woman to go through, and to accept that they've lost their womanhood. And in the meantime, your supposed 'man of God' gets an itch and decides to go catting around behind his devoted wife's back to score a little strange stuff on the side? Did Mentzer really think if he got caught and broke down in tears like Jimmy fricken Swaggart, that all would be forgiven? Maybe in your good book it would, but not in mine, Pastor."

Harkin glared at me. “All right,” he said, holding up his hand in protest. “You made your point. So what do you want exactly? How much hush money? You know, we don’t have a fortune like the Catholic church.”

“No,” I acknowledged. “But you must have enough that Sommers wants to sink his fangs into you. That’s what I want to know. Why is he so adamant to merge, and why are you so willing to give in?”

Harkin sighed, looked down at his hands, and took a deep breath, like it was going to be painful for him to talk about it.

“He’s been after us for a while,” he said wearily. “Trying to coerce us into joining forces with him. In reality though, we wouldn’t be joining him as much as becoming subservient. Sure, he says that we would all get to keep our positions and so forth, but in reality, we’d become nothing more than figureheads for him to use. Most of our voting power would be stripped away, and we’d just be his pawns.”

“How do you know that? I asked. “How do you know that would be the outcome if you merged with him?”

“Because that’s what happened to other churches that went with Pathways.”

“It’s happened to others?”

“Yes,” Harkin said.

“Okay,” I said. “For the time being, let’s just focus on what’s happening to your church, to God’s Way. Tell me the whole thing, start to finish.”

Harkin let out a big breath of air and pushed his plate of food toward the center of the table.

"Like I said, Sommers has been after us for a while to merge with him. Roy had always politely turned him down, and Sommers tried to act magnanimous about it - even though you could tell he was irked. He even offered to help us with our website as a gesture of good will. We accepted, and his wife came in with a couple of software gurus to try to jazz it up a bit."

"And…"

"And everything seemed to be going fine until Roy died, or, as you claim—"

"Committed suicide, Pastor Harkin," I said. "It's on my video, and it's irrefutable. Pastor Roy Mentzer took his own life. I'm sorry."

"Thanks," he said, grimacing. I could see his eyes moisten a bit.

"Anyway, it was only a couple of days afterward that Sommers showed up to my office. He closed the door and played a video for me that showed Roy in a very sinful manner. He said that he received it from an anonymous source, and that probably the best thing we could do would be to join his church."

"Provide you cover, right?" I offered.

"Exactly. But I could tell that he didn't want to protect us, he wanted to *own* us. He was just trying to avoid saying it."

"Has anyone else in the church seen the video? Any of the other pastors or members of the board?"

"Oh no," Harkin responded adamantly. "I've kept it under wraps so far, and I'd like to keep it that way. Church people - and even pastors and elders, are no different than others when it comes to keeping a secret. The more people know about it, the greater the chance it could leak out."

"Smart move," I said, admiring Harkin for his acumen. "So you're shouldering this burden by yourself then?"

"Jesus would have," he said evenly and I didn't bite.

"Where do you think he got the video?" I asked.

"I figured he must have gotten so desperate to have us merge with him, that he hired a private investigator to follow Roy around in the hopes that he could catch him doing something illicit."

"Possibly," I said. "PIs are used all the time for that sort of thing."

"And so between Roy's suicide, and what's on this video, Sommers can ruin us if he wants to," Harkin said.

"Maybe," I admitted. "But have you ever thought about just telling Sommers to go fly a kite and do whatever he wants to with the video? You'll have to take your lumps in the media, and it will be a scandal, but the church could eventually recover, couldn't it? Isn't forgiveness one of your chief mantras?"

"Yes," Harkin said. "And maybe the church could recover, but I don't know if Betty Mentzer could. She's very fragile, and she's already devastated. I don't think she would be able to take another blow like this. For the rest of her life, she'd have to live with the fact that people would know that Roy, a man of the cloth, had left her to find someone else more desirable."

Harkin looked up at me with a pleading look in his eyes. "I can't do that do her," he said desperately. "Or to her kids. I have to protect them."

The waitress came by just then and looked at our unfinished plates.

"I'm sorry," she said. "Was there something wrong with your meals?"

Before Harkin had to speak, I handled it.

"No," I said easily. "It was great. I guess we just weren't as hungry as we thought we were."

"Hmmm," she murmured as she picked up the two plates, balancing them deftly on her forearm. "Any room for dessert, or coffee then?"

"Coffee, please," I said and glanced at Harkin.

He looked up at her. "Just coffee for me as well."

She walked away and I looked back at Harkin.

"So what's on the video that Sommers showed you?" I asked.

Harkin shook his head sadly. "Roy and some woman, checking into a cheap motel. It…it looks pretty bad."

I stared at Harkin dumbfounded; it couldn't be…

"Don't tell me," I said. "Redheaded woman, the Starlite Motel?"

Harkin shook his head in amazement. "How did you - "

"Because I might have the same video, probably shot on the same day."

"What?"

"My sentiments exactly," I said. "Do you have access to the video close by? Can I see it? Then I can tell you."

Harkin pulled out his phone and said, "I have it on here. But I'd like to see yours as well."

The waitress returned with two cups of steaming coffee and set them down in front of us. When she was gone, I continued.

"All right," I agreed, pulling out my own phone. I navigated to a secure cloud server I used to store files and queued up the video. "Just press play," I said.

We exchanged phones, and began watching each other's version of the final, incontrovertibly damning moments of Pastor Roy Mentzer's life.

After only a few seconds of watching, the fog suddenly lifted in my brain. It was all clear now. It *was* the same video, shot the same day. I watched the brief exchange between Red and Mentzer, and him tripping on the curb going into the room. More importantly, by the angle of the shot, I could tell the video had to have been shot from only one place - Reds car.

Damn it! I thought. The visor; a tiny camera concealed into it. Red hadn't been checking her makeup in the mirror before she went into the room; she had been turning on the camera. How could I have not caught it?

"I can't believe it," Harkin said, hitting the pause button on the video. "Virtually the same video, but I see the woman's car in your video. Mine doesn't have that."

"I know," I said. "Because your video was shot from a visor cam…in that woman's car. By any chance, do you recognize the woman in the video?"

"No," Harkin said. "But I recognize the car."

"You do?"

Harkin nodded.

"Yes. It belongs to Pastor Sommers' wife."

TWELVE

My mind flashed back to Sommers' wife at the funeral service for Mentzer, and I tried to do a quick mental comparison: same build, same height… a good wig, glasses, and a hat would make her all but unrecognizable to everyone except those who had access to facial recognition software - which I did. In my gut, I just knew that it was her. Harkin caught on just then.

"Wait a minute," he said. "You don't think that this is Sommers' wife, do you?"

I nodded. "I do. And I'd be willing to bet money on it."

Harkin was dumbfounded.

"You mean, he would have his own wife sleep with another man? Just to get his hands on his church?"

"No. Not exactly," I said. "Your video only shows them going into the room. Hit play on my phone again and watch what happens. And I didn't edit it. It's continuous as you can see by the counter."

Harkin resumed watching the video, all the way up to the point where Pastor Roy, tortured and disillusioned, got into his car to drive off and kill himself.

"You can stop it now," I said. "You don't really want or need to see any more."

Harkin terminated the video, and set my phone on the table in front of me.

"I'll take your word for it," he said. Then added, "Thanks."

"So as you can see, Sommers' wife didn't have sex with Pastor Roy. There was no time to even get undressed. But she didn't need to sleep with him to get what they wanted".

"A video of a man entering a motel room with another woman."

"Exactly. Try to explain that to your wife or significant other. I figured that Red - I mean Sommers' wife - was a pro and that she had just ripped him off. Now I know better."

"So what did happen that day then?" Harkin asked.

I paused for a moment and took a long sip on my coffee.

"After they got the video footage that they needed, they - meaning Sommers and his wife, put the screws to Roy that he was going to have give up his church or else they would leak the video of him going into the room."

"You mean she confronted him that day about it?"

"Yes. That's my guess. But I doubt very much that she did it in person. Did you see him holding a note in his hand?"

Harkin nodded.

"I noticed it, yes."

"They probably had a note already made out with their threat. After all, no need to get into a verbal confrontation. Sommers' wife - who by the way is in a disguise so that she can't be identified on the video - lures him to the motel, gets the footage she needs, and then leaves him the note, demanding he play ball or else."

Harkin put his head into his hands and slowly shook it.

"Poor Roy," he said. "He must have felt that he had no way out, and that he was going to lose God's Way, the very thing he had worked so long and hard for. He couldn't stand the thought of it."

"Exactly. And I'm sure that Sommers and his wife hadn't planned on Roy taking himself out of the picture."

"And so they had no choice but to go to me, the next in command."

"Yes."

"So what now?" Harkin asked, "We're going to have to go ahead with it, right? We have to merge with Pathways or else Roy and his family will be forever shamed."

"No," I said, turning to look at Harkin. "But you're going to have to help me if you want me to save Gods Way Church."

* * *

For the next hour, I pumped Harkin about everything he could tell me about Sommers' church. Over the course of several cups of coffee, we had shifted from being adversaries, to allies. Harkin made no bones about the fact that Pathways was huge in the area - and beyond. They had satellite churches, called campuses, spread out all over Los Angeles and Orange counties, and they were renowned for doing a lot of "The Lord's work."

"Such as what?" I asked.

"They have quite a missionary force overseas," Harkin explained. "And a good portion of their money goes into building schools, hospitals, and so forth in various third-world countries."

"Something that would take a lot of resources," I observed.

Harkin nodded. "It sure does. We have a couple of small missions in Africa, and one in the Appalachians, but nothing on the scale of what Pathways does. It's huge."

"And they got huge because they continue to absorb other churches?" I offered.

"Yes. Some of their membership has increased the old-fashioned way, by getting more and more congregates, but that only takes you so far and is painstaking.

"A handful here and there," I said.

"Right. But if you absorb another church like ours - "

"Then you pick up thousands of members, *and* their tithing, all in one fell swoop," I said.

Harkin looked at me and nodded. We were both quiet for a long while, our guts overflowing with coffee, and our brains deluged with the magnitude of Pathways' devious machinations. Finally, I had enough of my own reverie and went back into intelligence gathering mode.

"So how many churches would you say Pathways has merged with?" I asked.

"Three other churches that I know of," Harkin answered.

"Has anyone ever been successful at resisting the pressure to join Pathways that you know of?"

"I don't know if you could call it successful, but Pastor Bill Williams from The United Spirit Church had supposedly been leaned on quite heavily by Sommers to join Pathways. He never caved in, but then all of a sudden a video that showed him entering a hotel room with a strange woman somehow found its way to the news media."

"Don't tell me - a redhead?"

Harkin reflected on it for a moment and I could tell he was reaching back into his memory.

"I can't say for sure," he admitted. "It seems to me that she was. It would certainly fit the pattern."

I didn't belabor the fact and moved on.

"So what happened then to this Pastor…ah…?"

"Williams. It was a huge scandal and he was shamed. His wife left him, and he ended up being booted out by his own church."

"Did his church eventually join Pathways in the end?"

"Yes."

"So it's not exactly a happy ending," I offered.

"No, and I don't want to see ours go the same way."

"It won't," I said. "What's your deadline with Sommers? When did he say he'd publicize the video if God's Way didn't play ball?"

"He gave me until the end of the month - which is only three and a half weeks away - or else he was going public with it. He said there is a lot of The

Lord's work to do, and that he needs all the support he can get."

"Pathways may be calling what they do the Lord's work," I said wryly. "But I'd say it's more of The Devil's work."

"Yes it is," Harkin agreed emphatically.

"And you know what, Pastor Harkin?"

"What?"

"The Devil just met his match," I said.

THIRTEEN

Tiffany stepped around the car slowly, touching it, feeling its sleek lines. There was no doubt that it was a beauty, and looked as if it were going Mach 3 when it was standing still.

We were standing in the driveway of our house. I had just come home with my new DB9 Carbon edition Aston Martin. The car made extensive use of carbon fiber material in its sleek construction and was flat black in color. Under the hood was no less impressive, and the vehicle sported a naturally aspirated V-12 engine that pumped out over five hundred horsepower. The DB9 had a top speed of one-hundred-eighty mph, and could get to sixty from a standing start in just a little over four seconds. It was more testosterone on four wheels than I had ever seen before.

"Nice car, Jack," Tiffany said breezily, her hand gently caressing the carbon fiber side strakes.

"So what? Are you going through a midlife crisis?" she giggled. "That's so passé."

"Ha, ha," I retorted. "This is just honey to catch the bees."

"Hmm. Honey huh?" She gestured to the ring finger on my left hand. I was sporting a plain gold wedding band on it.

"And I see that you got married too. So that does that mean you already caught a bee?"

"Not yet," I said. "But I intend to. The ring is just more honey."

"Uh-huh," Tiffany said warily.

"You want to take a walk?" I said. "I'll explain it all."

A few minutes later, we were heading south from Manhattan Beach and walking on the concrete strand that separates the beach sand from the multi-million dollar homes that abut it. As we strolled hand in hand, I caught Tiffany up with my activities of the past couple of days: My meeting with Harkin, how Gods Way was being extorted into merging with Pathways, the second video of Mentzer and Red, and how Red was actually Sommers' wife.

"You're kidding?" Tiffany cried incredulously. "You're sure of it?"

"Absolutely," I said. "I used facial recognition software and analyzed the image from the video I shot to that of an image of Sommers' wife I found on their web page. Her name is Belinda, by the way."

"Which means *very beautiful*," Tiffany offered.

I felt my head jerk around to look at her.

"It does?" I said, stunned.

"Yes."

"How do you know?"

Tiffany shrugged nonchalantly.

"You learn these things when you start looking into stage names," she said easily.

"Hmmm," I murmured, impressed.

"So anyway, I used my software and it analyzed her chin, jaw, nose, etceteras and came up with a ninety-eight percent probability, which is good enough for me. That, added to the fact that Sommers would probably not want to involve any more people than absolutely necessary in his little scheme, made me realize that his wife is indeed the notorious femme fatale - aka Red."

"So this Sommers would actually pimp out his wife to grow his church?" Tiffany asked.

"Who knows what extent these guys will go to?" I said. "Most of them believe they're on a mission from God, and that the end justifies the means."

"That's sick!" Tiffany hissed.

"True," I admitted. "But it's not just men of the cloth who have become seduced by their own megalomaniac dreams. You remember John D. Rockefeller?"

"The guy who started Standard Oil?"

"Yes. He was a very devoutly religious man who actually believed that God had put him on earth to do good things. And he *did* accomplish lots of incredible charity work: building hospitals, universities, museums, and so forth. But he needed vast amounts of money to do it. So along the way, he was a ruthless tyrant who would stop at nothing to control the oil industry. He destroyed companies, people's lives, and used all sorts of illegal methods to get what he wanted."

"Because God told him it was okay?"

"Yep. God had bigger plans and old John D couldn't be bothered with playing by the rules. And I think Sommers is the same way."

"Even to the point of selling his wife's flesh?" Tiffany asked.

"He didn't have to. Remember the video I showed you of them at the motel. Pastor Roy couldn't have even gotten his pants down in the time they were in there."

"True. But still, the idea that you're using your wife to entice other men."

"I agree," I said. "Pretty low. And probably not the first time it's been done by one of these guys."

Then I added, "But I want to make it's the last time Pathways ever does it."

Tiffany laughed just then.

"What's so funny?" I asked.

"The idea of you helping a church."

I laughed myself. "I know," I said. "Strange bed-fellows huh? No pun intended."

"And I'm going to help you, Jack," Tiffany blurted out suddenly.

"No way," I said emphatically.

"Listen Jack, I can -"

"No," I said more stridently. "You know that I don't ever want you to get involved in my work."

"But…"

"But nothing! And, you have your tour coming up."

"I can postpone it," Tiffany pleaded. "It's no big deal really."

I knew that it *was* a big deal and that she had been working hard to book this tour for quite some time. We stepped down the walkway at the border of

Hermosa and Manhattan Beach to get to the lower strand, and I was saved momentarily from continuing our debate.

Built right onto the corner of Thirty-fifth Street and The Strand was the famous *90210* house from the iconic TV show from the 1990s. A two-story, blue, white, and gray 3670- square-foot cape cod. It was probably the most photographed home in the area. As if supporting the claim, a young couple were standing out in front of it trying to take a selfie with their phone at that very moment.

"Excuse me," the young girl asked when she spotted Tiffany and me. "Could you please take our picture?"

"Sure," I said, and took the girl's phone. I snapped a couple of photos of them mugging it up for their friends to see, and then Tiffany and I continued on.

"Listen Tiffany," I said. "I really appreciate your wanting to help, but this is a cakewalk for me and you know it. I'll get the goods on Pathways and then I'll tell them they are going to lay off Gods Way Church and any others. No sweat."

She was quiet and we stopped to stare out at the Pacific. The sun was starting to go down and it looked like it was going to be a nice sunset. Other couples and individuals were doing the same thing, some capturing the magic on their phones. I put my arm around Tiffany's waist and pulled her close to me. I was glad to feel that she didn't resist.

Without turning to me, she asked in a voice that I knew was shaded with disappointment that she wouldn't be part of the festivities, "So when are you going to start on this?"

"Tomorrow," I said. "Harkin is on a deadline from Sommers, and I don't want to see it come and go. I've got to work fast."

"And just what is your *work* going to consist of?" Tiffany asked.

"Pathways is going to meet one of their juiciest new benefactors…and they're going to snare him in their web of seduction."

Tiffany turned to me. "Not before I do," she said.

Then she gave me a nice long kiss.

FOURTEEN

If the God's Way Church of the late Pastor Roy Mentzer was nice, the Pathways Church blew it away in just about every manner of luxury and opulence. Situated on eight acres in the bedroom community of Torrance, the modern steel and glass facility housed seven buildings with a combined square footage of over 200,000 square feet. In addition to the 50,000-square-foot main sanctuary, there were buildings for teen ministries, women's ministries, men's ministries, senior's ministries, and virtually every other program under the sun to salvage or augment the spirit. They had extensive media and television presence, and their sermons were beamed worldwide to over thirty countries, with a total viewership of close to 100,000 souls.

As with God's Way, I had first scoured the church's website for info and found that it was similar to the other church websites I had seen. It had the requisite *About Us*, *Our Leadership*, *Services,* and *Donation* pages, but it also had a tab that directed the visitor to a *Lord's Work* page. Here, broken down by geographic area, was information on the various projects that Pathways was involved in: a new school in southern Sudan, a sewage treatment plant in Chad, an orphanage in Honduras. All worthy causes, and all in some of the world's most volatile countries. In the lingo of those on the front lines, these were referred to as *danger-zone missions.* The page contained descriptions of the various projects, as well as photos, and even some videos from the locations.

I clicked on one of the videos, and it appeared to be from Chad and taken at night. A man of about thirty stood facing the camera with a microphone in his hand. In the background, floodlights illuminated an array of pipes, scaffolding, and electrical conduit. It was clearly taken from a work in progress construction site, and the man beamed as he gave a play-by-play of the recent progress that had been made. Sommers' voice could be heard offscreen, asking the man specific questions about the project and praising the group's efforts. I guessed that the video might have been, at one point, a live feed that may have been beamed straight to Pathways so the congregates could bask in their church's far-reaching accomplishments.

After I finished watching the video, I navigated to Google Earth and saw that the roof of the Pathways' main sanctuary in Torrance supported several large satellite dishes. That would help explain the live feed. I guessed that they had sophisticated IP satellite video streaming equipment at their many missions throughout the world as a way to not only keep real-time tabs on the progress, but also to showcase all of The Lord's work that they were doing.

The satellite imagery also showed a large opening in the middle of the Pathways building that, based on the amount of green I saw, must have been a garden atrium. Most surprisingly, the roof of the main ministry also contained a heliport. I checked aviation records and found that Pathways leased an Augusta A109; a sleek, $3 million state-of-the-art airship with seating for seven. The whirlybird must have been used to whisk Pastor Sommers off at a moment's notice to grace, with his presence, his many other subsidiary campuses throughout the area. From the image, I clicked to *Street View* and took a snoop around the parking lot of the church. Not surprisingly, the lot was filled with scores of Bimmers, Benzs, Porsches, and other high-end vehicles.

Harkin had told me, in no uncertain terms, that spiritually speaking this wasn't the backwater of the south, and that the self-sacrificing suffering message just wouldn't play with the affluent congregates of the South Bay. Borrowing a page from the New Age playbook of some of the other mega-churches, Sommers preached a gospel that embraced success and the building of personal wealth. As long as you tithed generously to Pathways, you could pass GO, collect your two hundred dollars, and continue right on to Boardwalk or Park Place guilt free.

The most interesting thing of all was the info, or rather the dearth of it, that I could dig up on Sommers and his wife. It was like they had fallen out of the sky and landed in the South Bay of Los Angeles, ready to hang out their shingle. I asked Zahid to try to dig further, but he didn't come up with much. To me it was the welcomest news of all; it meant the good pastor and his wife probably had something to hide.

I parked the Aston Martin in a nice conspicuous spot near the main entrance to the church and stepped through a set of large glass doors into the reception area. The interior was modern, spacious, and airy. The floor was done in Rosa Aurora marble tiles, and fancy trim and expensive artwork adored the high walls. It seemed like I was stepping into a modern art museum, rather than a church.

An attractive woman in her forties smiled at me as I stepped through the front doors. She was seated at a large curved receptionist desk, about the size of Turn One at Talladega. I approached and informed her that Jack Donaldson had arrived to meet with Pastor Sommers.

She consulted her monitor briefly, and I was directed to take a seat in one the oversized white leather chairs in the reception area. I went to the closest one and was swallowed by it, as much as sat on it.

While I was waiting to see the man himself, I noticed the security camera domes in the high ceiling overhead. Judging by the number and placement, they had good coverage of the reception area and I wondered just how paranoid Sommers and his entourage were.

A few moments later Sommers stepped out from behind a door leading into the reception area. He was dressed like a million bucks in a custom-tailored dark gray suit, and Ferragamo shoes that probably cost as much as a new refrigerator. I rose to meet him and we shook hands. I noticed that his grip was warm and firm.

"How are you doing, Mr. Donaldson?" Sommers beamed, and I could tell he was sizing me up.

I'm sure that even churches got their share of crackpots and phonies, and so I had Zahid pull out all of the stops and do a major bit of sock-puppetry on the Internet to create a tempting persona for me. After I made the initial contact, I'm sure Sommers' organization had done at least a cursory search to determine that I wasn't a nutcase, and that they had in fact, stumbled upon a potential treasure to rival that of the Lost Dutchman mine.

Jack Donaldson was the husband of Patricia Donaldson, nee Reynolds, whose father, James "Bud" Reynolds, had made a fortune in the early days of the dot-com boom. One day, old man Reynolds disappeared without a trace while flying his plane to his private island in the Caribbean. After a several months-long exhaustive search, Reynolds was declared dead in absentia, and his only daughter, Patricia, a hopeless spinster, became the sole heir to the late magnate's fortune.

Chronically overweight and plain in appearance, Patricia was nonetheless inundated with sympathetic suitors vying to sweep her off her feet and to shower her with all of the love and affection that she so rightfully deserved. And of all the scoundrels waiting in the wings, yours truly, the dashing, albeit roguish Jack Donaldson, was the only paramour given the nod - as long as I would sign a prenup.

"So you're interested in working with Pathways to help us in our mission of spreading the word and doing The Lord's work, Mr. Donaldson?" Sommers asked.

Now that we were standing toe-to-toe, I got a better look at the pastor, and it was easy to see why he was the spiritual leader to thousands of devoted followers. He was at least six-two and seemed to be in good fighting trim. His face was nicely tanned with only a few wrinkles and crows-feet, and I wouldn't have been surprised to find out that he had regular work done. His hair was dark brown with just a wisp of gray at the temples. It was thick and full, and most importantly, it was all his. His eyes were blue, and they seemed to sparkle as he smiled. If the religion business didn't work out for him, I'm sure the telegenic Sommers could always find his way to the anchor desk on the evening news.

"Yes," I said. "We're considering it, at least."

"Oh," Sommers said, feinting surprise. He glanced down to my left hand and made of show of spotting my wedding band. "I didn't know that you were married Mr. Donaldson. Will your wife be involved in your work with us?"

"I'm sure she will be eventually," I said. "But not for a while. She's in Europe right now and won't be back for a couple of months. I'm out on kind of a fact-finding mission. We're looking at several different institutions to see which one will be the best fit for us."

And then, I couldn't resist the temptation to add, "Pretty much, to get the best bang for our buck."

At the comment, I couldn't help but notice the tiniest of smirks cross Sommers' face. "Well, I'm sure you'll see that Pathways can deliver on that for you," he said confidently.

He gestured toward the door he had entered from.

"Let's go into my office, shall we?" he said.

The receptionist pushed an unseen button and the door out of reception area clicked open. Sommers and I stepped through it and that's when I saw the first of them... bodyguards. One was right inside the door and another was down the hall. They looked like secret service aides and had the same high-grade discreet earpiece worn by the men who protected the president. Maybe these guys thought they had an even higher calling, or at least I'm sure that's what Sommers had convinced them of.

Unlike the cold marble floors of the reception area, the interior of the building was all plush wall-to-wall carpeting, in blood red. The interior walls were faux painted to the color and look of distressed leather, and the lemon yellow baseboard and chair-rail moldings gave a nice effect. More artwork; some modern, some impressionist, graced the walls.

With a bodyguard discreetly in tow, we moved down the hallway and into Sommers' private office, which was as lavish as any I had seen in executive suites. It was at least thirty feet by thirty feet, and I smelled leather, wood, and unbridled power as we stepped inside. Floor to ceiling windows covered nearly an entire wall of the room with one of the windows apparently a slider. It looked out into the atrium I had seen on Google Earth, and contained a lush fern garden with crushed seashell pathways, and a large rock waterfall as its centerpiece. The same blood red carpeting in the hallways covered the expansive floor space of the office. Tall bookcases that might have been made from ebony wood flanked the ends of the room. Besides holding an impressive collection of leather-bound tomes, the bookcases also held African sculptures, Chinese pottery, and several framed and matted pictures of Sommers posing with celebrities and several politicians. A massive desk, large enough to land an aircraft on, and made of the same wood as the bookcases, sat in the center of the room, and huge double doors made of mahogany, with large silver crosses inset in them, closed off the chamber from the outside world.

Sommers excused the bodyguard, and then closed the doors. He motioned me to a chair on the opposite side of his desk, and I sat down and noticed the silver framed portrait of he and his wife sitting on the desk and angled toward me. It was a great shot of two beautiful people looking resplendent as they flashed thousand-watt smiles and beaming as if they owned the world, which maybe someday they would.

Sommers sat down across from me, adjusted his suit coat, and was just starting to speak, when something caught his attention. He stared briefly at a large computer monitor on his desk and his eyes squinted like he was reading something. He looked up at me apologetically.

"I'm sorry, Mr. Donaldson," he said mournfully. "I have a situation that requires my immediate attention. Could you just indulge me a few minutes?"

"Absolutely," I said. "The Lord's work never rests, does it?"

"No," he laughed. "I'm afraid it doesn't."

He got up and left the office, closing the door behind him.

As I sat waiting patiently for the pastor to return, I wondered just how many cameras and microphones were on me at that very minute, recording my every move and sound. I didn't give any indication that I was considering the possibility of being watched, and instead pulled out my phone, pretending to check messages.

While I played my charade, I considered just what sort of urgent business Sommers had that he had to leave a potentially plenteous fish waiting on the line. Would he be so reckless as to have someone of my philanthropical bent slip away from him to share my bounty elsewhere?

I barely had time to ponder the situation when Sommers returned a few minutes later, immediately dispelling the notion that he was going to let this prize get away. Instead, he proved to me indisputably that he wanted to make sure to sink the hook deeply into this fish, and then reel it in and land it.

"I'm sorry, Mr. Donaldson," he said. "Is there any way I could have you meet with my wife, Belinda?"

FIFTEEN

Sommers himself escorted me down the hallway to Belinda's private office. As if on cue, or with hearing that could rival that of a bat, she opened an identical silver-cross-inlaid door before we could even knock.

"Hello," she said warmly. Her voice had a bit of southern accent, syrupy and sweet. It was a voice you could either trust or fear.

We shook hands; hers was slender, dry, and cool to the touch. Her blond hair was done up the in the same style I had seen it at God's Way Church and now that we were closer, I could see that her eyes were a sparkling emerald green.

She was dressed in a pale pink, light wool suit that I think was from the latest Armani collection. The jacket was a single button, with notched lapels and welted pockets. Under the jacket she wore a silk blouse in bone, and below the waist, a pencil skirt of the same pink shade. The hemline was a few inches above the knee, and the skirt was slit on either side.

Her silk hose were nude in color, and she wore a pair of suede pumps that were an exact match for her suit. A pearl station necklace accented her slender neck, and she had on a wedding ring with a flawless diamond that probably was the equivalent of the GDP of some third-world countries.

"Thank-you dear," the pastor breathed, as if his wife had just pulled him from a burning building.

Belinda Sommers waved a perfectly manicured hand breezily.

"I know, I know," she teased playfully. "He's *so* busy," she laughed, turning toward me. "Always has some business to attend to."

Sommers chuckled heartily, and then they gave each other an air kiss before he moved on back down the hall.

"Please come in," Belinda said, sweeping her willowy arm through the open doorway.

I entered and she closed the door solidly behind us. As it was clicking shut, I grabbed a quick look around.

Her office was smaller than her husband's was, but it was still nicely done and with high-quality furnishings and floor coverings that left no doubt that there were no expenses spared. The furniture was solid teak, and she had several expensive Persian rugs covering the blood red carpeting under her desk, and hanging from the walls. On either side of her desk were sliding glass doors that looked out into the same atrium and fern garden. I did a quick calculation of the spatial distances and layout of the two offices, and wondered if Sommers could see in.

I realized after a second that my worries were misguided and that with the network of cameras

Pathways had in place, why would he resort to such a low-tech way of snooping? I'm sure Belinda's office had surveillance equipment, and all her husband had to do to keep tabs on her was to pull up the correct monitor.

Belinda pointed to a conference table with eight chairs around it that was positioned in front of one of the sliding glass doors.

"Let's sit over here if it's okay?" she said. "I think the desk is just so formal."

I nodded and we moved over to the table.

I pulled out a chair on the side of the table and sat down, leaving the power one on the end for her. She pulled out the chair, but then surprised me by pulling it away from the table and rolling it next to mine so that I had to turn to face her. We were so close that I could smell her perfume, which admittedly, had started to arouse me. It probably contained high levels of pheromones. She crossed her legs, and picked up a steno notepad and pen from the table. Her legs were gorgeous, and she made no effort to pull down her skirt, which had already hiked up a few inches.

"So then, Mr. Donaldson…" she began.

"Jack," I interrupted.

She smiled, and I stared into a set of pearly whites that could make a small fortune advertising for teeth-brightening products.

"Jack," she corrected herself. "I understand you want to fund one of our missions, or to start a foundation with Pathways?"

"Yes," I said. "My wife and I are exploring those options."

"Oh," she exclaimed, surprised, and I wondered if Belinda and her husband had studied under the same drama coach. "Should she be part of this meeting?"

"That's okay," I said easily. "She's in Europe right now."

"Should we wait for her to get back?"

"That's okay," I said. "She's shopping for antiques."

I gave a thin smirk, and then added, "And she won't be home for several months."

At this mention of the cat being away, I detected the tiniest bit of a coquettish smile crossed Belinda Sommers' lips. Her emerald green eyes dilated ever so slightly.

"I see," she said slowly.

"And she's entrusted me to look into the various organizations and determine which one might be the best fit."

Getting back on track, she opened her notebook and clicked the pen open. In doing so, she leaned forward just ever so slightly. "Can I ask what other organizations you've spoken with Jack?"

"I'm sorry," I said. "No. I've been asked to maintain discretion, and I know how to keep a secret."

She looked over at me and smiled again. I didn't know if she was thrilled, or disappointed in hearing me say it.

"I understand," she said evenly. "So let me ask you this, what do you already know about Pathways and what we do?"

"I had to resist the temptation to say, *a hell of a lot more than you realize,* but simply answered,

"Mostly what is on your website. Why don't you give me the rundown Mrs. Sommers?"

Now it was her turn to correct me and put us both on more familiar terms.

"Belinda," she smiled, and she leaned closer still.

"Belinda," I repeated, and we both sat staring at each other and smiling. She uncrossed, then re-crossed her legs, giving me a nice show in the process.

Finally, she broke the spell, and for the next fifteen minutes gave me a beautiful sales pitch about the history of Pathways, their mission, and how much of The Lord's work they were able to accomplish. She made a special effort to emphasize that Pathways, was able to uniquely accomplish their mission when others, such as smaller ministries - and especially our government - were so ineffectual. She also suggested that I attend the service that Sunday so I could watch the live feed from one of their missions and bear witness myself to the miracles being performed around the world everyday by Pathways. Throughout her delivery of this impassioned soliloquy, I noted that she had slowly, and ever so stealthily, moved her chair closer and closer to me.

When she had finished and was catching her breath, I nodded heartily and said, "I see. So Pathways, because of their efficiency and resources, is able to accomplish what many others just can't seem to."

"Exactly!" she exclaimed, reeling back in her chair and clapping her hands as if I had just won the grand prize on a game show. "And with the generous support from unselfish individuals such as you - I mean, you and your wife, Pathways can do even more and spread The Lord's work even farther and wider than anyone could ever, ever imagine!"

I nodded and looked out the sliding glass door in her office, acting as if I was considering the incredible gravity of what she had just said.

When I turned back to her, I noticed her eyes seemed to be frozen on me. Instead of hopeful though, they appeared saucy, even sexually hungry. She leaned forward and placed her hand on top of mine.

"It would be really great to have you come into our family, and to work closely with you," she said in a breathy voice.

I met her gaze and kept it for a while. I let my eye slip down to her exposed legs for a brief moment, then looked back up. I wanted her to notice. She did, and I noted that her expression hadn't changed.

"Why don't you attend on Sunday?" she practically purred. "I would love to see you again."

"Likewise," I said, never taking my eye off hers.

* * *

One of the Pathways goons escorted me from Belinda's office back to the reception area. I walked through the door, bid a farewell to the receptionist, and then stepped outside into the bright sun.

I got into the Aston Martin and fired up the V-12, enjoying its throaty rumble. In a lot of ways, the machine was like the Sommers duo; sexy, powerful, and if not handled properly, dangerous.

I pulled out of the lot and started heading back toward Manhattan Beach and home. I had only gone half a mile, when an alarm went off in the car. It was my RF scanner alerting me; someone had put a GPS tracking device on my car.

SIXTEEN

I pulled into the first gas station I could find and parked the Aston Martin off to the side of the lot. I turned up the sensitivity of the RF scanner, got out of the car, and within a few minutes had located the device. It was tucked up on the inside of the frame and held in place by magnets. I pried it off and brought it back into the car with me.

It was one of the cheaper devices and I could have just tossed it in the trashcan at the station. Instead, I connected my phone to it and launched an app called *BreadCrumbs* that was designed to reprogram it.

As part of the profile Zahid had created for me, I - or rather my wealthy, absentee wife - owned a home in pricey Palos Verdes Estates. As soon as I had hacked into the GPS device, I plotted out a route that would have me at this gas station for a couple more minutes, followed by a quick stop at the grocery store, and then up to my mansion, where I would remain parked until tomorrow.

More than just plot out the route, the app looked at traffic lights, and historical speeds at certain times of the day, and took this data into account so that even to a trained observer it looked as if someone was just going about the regular errands of their day.

I depressed the key to initiate my wild goose chase, and then monitored it for a few minutes to make sure it was working as planned. In the meantime, I sent a text to remind myself to come up with new routes every day, and then to synch it for my return to Pathways on Sunday for the morning service. I knew that once my movements verified to them that I was who I said I was, they would sneak out to the parking lot while I was inside the church and remove it. I couldn't wait for The Lord's day to come.

Satisfied that my little red herring was indeed swimming in the stream for all the snoops at Pathways Church to see, I replaced the tracking device in the exact same spot under the car, and then continued on to my real home. You may be tricky Pathways; I'm just trickier.

* * *

The atmosphere at the Pathways Church on Sunday morning had a feeling of elegant pageantry to it. Besides being very well dressed, and bedecked with high-end jewelry and accessories, the congregation seemed to move about with a sense of style and grace that reminded me more of a Broadway opening or the Academy Awards, than a spiritual call to serve.

As I had expected, the lot was filled with high-end vehicles, and the mood in the crowd, as I moved through it, was upbeat. Granted, the congregates here had not just suffered the humiliating loss of their spiritual leader by his own hand as those at God's Way, but I got the sense that services at Pathways were more about high society socializing and networking than anything else. Instead of hearing holy words or bible verses recited, the focus of the conversations I overheard as I floated through were of money, both in the making and the spending of it.

"They're looking to go public."

"New Nordstrom's..."

"Here's my card. Let's touch bases next week."

"Vail this time of year..."

"Pebble Beach..."

"The new i8..."

I wondered how many fortunes got made, and how many business deals got hammered out, during The Lord's day at Pathways.

I had already taken a virtual tour by way of Pathways' website, but I still wanted to get a feel for the real thing. Besides the opulence of the marble-lined reception area, the rest of the church was equally as luxurious… and as secure.

I noticed cameras mounted overhead in the various rooms that I strolled through, as well as a couple of more stealthy security personnel. They were trying to blend in and be discrete, but a bouncer was a bouncer, and they all had a certain bearing to them.

At nine fifty-five an elegant chime sounded, and several sets of large double doors opened up. I didn't see any of the church muscle pushing them open, so I guessed them to be motorized. I also doubted if anyone had to stand by and sound the chime or push a button to open the doors. Like everything else about Pathways, it was state of the art and probably computer controlled.

At the sight of the portals beckoning, several people broke off their hoity-toity conversations and began moving into the main church. Some exchanged superficial hugs and air-kisses before heading in. Others glanced at their Rolex or Cartiers wondering, *where has all the time gone?*

I followed the well-heeled throng into the main ministry and took a spot closer to the front of the stage than I normally would for comfort; I wanted to make sure Sommers and his wife saw me there.

The interior of Pathways' main auditorium was close to twice as large as the one at God's Way. Their website stated that it could hold four thousand, and it appeared to be living up to the claim. It was also was at least twice as luxurious as God's Way. There was thick carpeting, of the same blood red color I had seen in the church's offices, as well as plush seating, and hanging from the ceiling overhead, three massive crystal chandeliers. A large electronic mixing board at the back of the room controlled the lighting, audio, and video for the chamber, and several monitors flanked the huge stage. An enormous video screen, as big as a garage door, and suspended by steel cables, hung down from the ceiling over center stage.

After several minutes, the band, which was larger and more complex than the symphonies of some US cities, began to play and to get the crowd warmed up with a quiet, instrumental piece. As they went through their opening number, I glanced around at the congregates. Some of them were listening politely, but others were trying to slyly work their phones, texting or e-mailing, possibly closing the deal they were negotiating only a few minutes prior.

My head was still turned away from the stage when I heard a female vocalist break into song. It was a beautiful, lilting voice, and it was one that I knew all too well. My head spun around angrily.

What the hell?

Tiffany was up on the stage, singing her heart out for Pathways Church.

SEVENTEEN

I sat stunned, feeling my anger rise higher the more I watched her. She had gone against me and had wormed her way into the organization in an attempt to help me. I didn't need her help and I had told her so. I pounded my fist into my thigh so hard it hurt. At the sound, several people in my row turned toward me.

As she belted out a great rendition of *How Great Thou Art*, Tiffany scanned the crowd, working it as any good performer would. When her eyes crossed over to me, she caught sight of my heated expression, and quickly averted her gaze. She was very good at moving on without making it appear obvious; probably from all of the practice she'd had dodging drunken Casanovas over the years.

I reminded myself then that I had to play it low-key as well, and hold my ire in check for the time being. I had a job to do, and wasting my attention and emotions on a situation that was out of my control would only be a waste of energy and a distraction.

There would be plenty of time when we got home to unleash the storm brewing inside of me.

After several songs had played through, it was time for the real show to kick off. Tiffany and the other band members stepped off the stage, and Pastor Ronald Sommers, looking resplendent in a dark-blue, single-breasted Valentino suit, strode out confidently from the wings. He moved with the grace and self-assurance of someone who was accepting the Nobel Prize, and his arrival triggered a standing ovation and nearly frenzied applause from the crowd. There was only one rock star in the room, and it was him, his outsized ego drinking it all in.

In the back, the video and audio crew pulled in on a tight shot of Sommers. All of the monitors showed his beaming face, his luminous smile. On the giant center screen, his head was nearly eight feet tall.

After reveling in the adoration for a few minutes, Sommers attempted to calm the crowd by taking his hands, palms down and motioning downward.

When the din finally subsided, he looked out to his adoring flock, visibly satisfied. He pulled a wireless microphone up to his mouth and said simply, "The Lord wants you to prosper."

The utterance of these words triggered an almost Pavlonian reaction from the crowd. More thunderous applause erupted, and several people jumped back up to their feet. The reverie died down on its own after a few moments, and then Sommers continued.

"The Lord wants you to live the good life, He wants you to have riches, and He wants to you to be rich, because He knows that if you are rich and prosperous…"

He paused to sweep an arm dramatically in an arc toward the crowd.

"…then we are *all* rich and prosperous."

This elicited still more applause.

"And when we are all rich and prosperous, the world itself becomes more prosperous. And when the world is more prosperous, our Lord and His world is more prosperous."

There was more applause, but Sommers muted it by continuing on.

"But please my brothers and sisters in God, *please* don't take my word for it. Take the word of our Lord himself."

On the display screens, a bible passage from II Corinthians 9:8 appeared.

"It's right here in the bible from the second Corinthians, 'And God is able to make all grace abound to you, so that having all sufficiency in all things at all times, you may abound in every good work.'"

"And, in James 1:4 'And let steadfastness have its full effect, that you may be perfect and complete, lacking in nothing.'"

I took a quick glance around at the crowd. Necks were craning forward, eyes wide open and pupils dilated. They were drinking it in. And why shouldn't they be? Sommers was giving them exactly what they wanted. By his fervent sermon and his focus on the good of prosperity, he was absolving them of their sins of greed and of coveting material goods. Whatever pangs of guilt they suffered for being successful, was being washed away. Pathways *and the bible* both told them it was okay to live in fancy homes, to drive fancy cars, to dine in the finest restaurants, and to dress themselves in the finest clothing.

Sommers himself was also scanning the crowd, enjoying the effect he was having on them. When he spotted me near the front, he eyed me for a long time, smiling a toothy grin. My mind flashed to the image of a hungry wolf, its canine incisors dripping with blood. I was sure that internally he was salivating at the thought of digging his fangs into my extensive, and more importantly, *vulnerable* wealth.

On an unseen cue, Belinda Sommers appeared at stage right and strode out toward her husband. Dressed in a beautiful and perfectly-tailored white suit, she looked every bit as dazzling as her husband. Leave it to her to pick a color that was the symbol of purity; there should have been a law.

They kissed and hugged briefly as she reached him, and then she took up a spot by his side. She looked up at him with admiration and then, bringing a microphone up to her mouth, turned to address the crowd.

"Pastor Sommers is right," she said emphatically. "The Lord is asking you, *begging* you, to be prosperous in this life. Because He knows…"

She turned to her husband.

"…He knows, and we know, that together, we can do more of His work. We can save more souls, provide more clean drinking water, and provide more health care than anyone else - including our own self-serving, liberal, tax and spend - "

"Wasteful tax and spend," Sommers interrupted.

"Yes," Belinda corrected herself, "*wasteful* tax and spend government in Washington and in Sacramento can *ever* do."

The last statement really hit a nerve with the crowd. They were on their feet again, roaring and applauding. Again, it didn't surprise me. Being conservative, most Christians sided with the Republican Party, a party that had built itself on a platform of lower taxes and less spending. Whether this was true or not was always subject to debate, but based on the obvious socioeconomic demographic of this crowd, it was easy to imagine that they were in the top income tax bracket. And they probably felt, like most successful people, that too much of their hard-earned income was being taken from them and squandered foolishly. Sommers let the pot boil for a few long moments, and then continued.

"And to show you again what Pathways is able to accomplish with the generous support of our congregation, of you, our brothers and sisters in God…"

He threw his hand up to his chest.

"…of our *saviors*, we would like to see if we could get an update from our own, Brother Bob, who at this very moment is in Southern Sudan and helping to accomplish The Lord's work, *all of our work*, by building a new school for the village."

"A *Christian* school," Belinda Sommers made a point to emphasize.

"Yes, a Christian school," Sommers agreed.

All of the screens in the capacious room switched to a deep blue color. On the screen, in white letters in the upper left corner were the words: "SAT - 112 ujk, acquiring."

In a few moments the screen changed to a pixilated, somewhat jerky image of a white man dressed in a khaki shirt and pants. He had sandy blond hair, and a full beard and mustache. He was standing, and facing the camera with a microphone to his mouth. It was dark in the background, and camera lights illuminated him, creating a halo of green around the edges of his blond hair. Behind him, we could see the faint outlines of the framework of a two-story building.

Sommers and his wife turned toward one of the side monitors so they could see it. The pastor turned back toward the crowd to get one last dig in at the politicians.

"And again, my brothers and sisters in God; we apologize for the quality of the video feed, our government, for all of the money they take from us, cannot seem to manage to provide us with better communication satellites."

A few chuckles bubbled up from the crowd, as well as some weary groans.

"Brother Bob?" Sommers said. "Can you hear us?"

There was a delay of about five seconds, and then we saw the man reach up to an earpiece he was wearing and press it against his ear.

"Yes," he said. "Pastor Sommers?"

"Yes Brother Bob," Sommers said. "We are all here, all of our brothers and sisters in God."

Belinda chimed in then.

"Hello Brother Bob," she said.

There was another delay of several seconds as we saw Brother Bob straining to listen. Finally, he answered back.

"Hello Belinda. How are you all doing?"

"We are doing fine, Brother Bob," Sommers said. "How are you? How is the school coming?"

Again, another delay. I took a quick sweep of the crowd to catch their expressions. They appeared to take the delay and the lack of fluidity of the presentation in stride.

"I'm fine," Brother Bob continued. "Fighting a bit of a cold, but we are doing great. We are making great progress here in South Sudan."

"Excellent!" Sommers and his wife chimed together.

"We had some troubles recently with getting material," Brother Bob explained. "And we kind of lost a few days, but The Lord provided, and we were able to make it up."

"Great!" the Sommers Siamese twins said in unison.

Brother Bob gestured to the area behind him and said, "I wish we had better lighting here, but you may be able to see behind me some of the new work that has gotten accomplished."

"We can, yes," Sommers assured him.

"And I've sent some still pictures from today," Brother Bob continued. "I'm not sure if you got them or not. If you have, you can show our brothers and sisters all of The Lord's work that they are accomplishing."

Sommers looked up at the control board expectantly and affirmation must have been given, because the displays changed to a photo of the building showing the raw framing and electrical wires. The roof sheeting had already been laid on top and a few shirtless workers wearing tool belts, presumably locals, were captured working in and around the structure.

Satisfied oohs and aahs emanated from the crowd.

"Brother Bob, can you still hear us?" Belinda asked.

"Yes, yes I can," we heard him say after a couple of seconds. "Do you have the picture up?"

"Yes, we do," Sommers said.

"This was from today," Brother Bob went on. "And you can see, we have the roof sheeted now, and we are working on the electrical."

After a few moments, Sommers nodded once again to the control board and the screens switched back to the live video feed.

"Great!" Sommers gushed. "Great work, Brother Bob. All of us back here - and I'm sure The Lord - are all very proud."

"Thank-you," Brother Bob said.

Belinda chimed in again.

"Bob, this is Belinda, thank-you as always for all of your hard work. You had better get to bed and take care of that cold. We know that it's the middle of the night there."

A few seconds later we saw Brother Bob nodding his head in agreement.

"Thank-you Belinda," he said. "I think I'll do that. Thank-you Pastor Sommers, and thank-you to the good generous people of Pathways Church. None of this would have been possible without you. God blesses you all."

"God bless you, Brother Bob," Sommers and his wife said in unison again, and I wondered if they finished each other's sentences. "Good-night."

"Good-night," we watched him say a few seconds later, before the screen pixilated again and changed back to the blue screen.

The band and Tiffany returned silently to the stage and took up their positions. In a few seconds, they were back at it and had launched into a dreamy rendition of *How Firm a Foundation*, with Tiffany leading them on vocals. I noticed that she resolutely was avoiding looking toward the area of the room where I was sitting.

Sommers, not wanting to lose the momentum of the moment, said, "And now my brothers and sisters in God, let's do some more of The Lord's work, *let's build that firm foundation!*"

The display screens changed to still images of construction projects interspersed with images of smiling African children, and of adults filled with the spirit and lifting their arms to the sky. Ushers appeared from out of nowhere at the ends of the aisles, and a velvet-lined wicker basket was passed from seat to seat. By the time it reached me, it was nearly close to overflowing with envelopes and cash, some with triple digit denominations.

I dropped in two $100 bills and passed the basket to the couple next to me. At the same time I looked up to see Belinda Sommers smiling at me. If she had winked, I wouldn't have been surprised.

* * *

The service ended a short time later, and like Gods Way Church, the Pathways disciples broke away to get refreshments, and to do more socializing and networking, before moving on to bible study classes or more targeted ministry services. I grabbed a cup of coffee from the café and continued strolling around. I looked for Tiffany in the crowd but didn't see her. Whether she was avoiding me because she didn't want to have to deal with my displeasure, or so that she didn't blow my cover, I couldn't say. She was at least that savvy.

"What did you think?" I heard a familiar female voice ask.

It was Belinda, who had come up from behind me.

"Very impressive," I said. "As you told me, a lot of The Lord's work is getting done."

"So then we can count on your support?" she smiled hopefully.

"It's very impressive, Mrs. Sommers," I said noncommittally.

"Belinda," she corrected me.

"I'm sorry, Belinda," I corrected myself. "But as I told you, I have other organizations to investigate, and I really need to make sure we're getting the best fit."

She stared at me, her mouth pouting. Instead of coming off as pitiful though, it appeared sexy, which I'm sure was the effect she was aiming for.

"I think that sometimes people just need to step away from everything for a bit, don't you agree?"

I didn't know exactly what she meant by that statement, or what leap of logic she was trying to connect the dots with, but I played along in her game.

"Yes," I said evenly.

"So maybe we need to have a more *private* conversation about your involvement with Pathways?" she said.

I nodded.

"So you can convince me?" I said slowly.

"Yes."

I stared at her a long time.

"And would you happen to know of a place where we could have 'more privacy?'"

She licked her lips ever so daintily.

"I sure do," she said.

EIGHTEEN

"Just what the hell do you think you're doing?" I said as soon as Tiffany stepped through the doorway of our kitchen.

She calmly set her purse down on the counter and grabbed a glass from the overhead cabinet.

"Helping you, Jack."

"I told you; I don't need any help."

She shook her head wearily.

"You are so stubborn."

Up to this point in our relationship, we had only had two arguments - about what, I couldn't remember at the moment - but I recalled the discomfort I felt each time.

She moved over to the refrigerator and pushed her glass against the swing arm built into the pocket in the door. Several ice cubes dropped into the glass.

"Maybe I am," I said. "But I thought we had an agreement that you would never get involved in my work?"

She filled the glass with water and took a long sip.

"Well, this is different," she said.

"Why is it different?"

"Because you yourself said that you had a deadline or else Sommers was going to spill the beans on Pastor Roy. I'd like to help you expedite the situation, so that the deadline doesn't come and go."

"I'm doing fine," I insisted, although I could hear the twinge of doubt in my own voice. I didn't like the idea of not having the luxury of unlimited time to deal with things.

Tiffany slammed the water glass on the granite countertop. "Oh really Jack?" she shot back. "And what exactly do you know about Pathways with only a couple of weeks left before that deadline? Just what you learned on the web, and what Harkin told you, and not much else. I can get you the inside info that you need."

"I'm completely capable of getting all the info I need," I said, noticing that the volume of my voice had risen.

"From who Jack? Zahid?" Tiffany demanded. "He can't get you the dirt that I can by poking around on the web."

"And what dirt might that be?"

"Dirt like Tim Bennett."

"I know that name," I said. "He's - "

"The chief operations officer for Pathways," Tiffany completed my statement.

"Right."

I thought back to some of the primary research I had done on Pathways' organization. Bennett's face and bio were on their website under "Staff," along with the directors of communications, maintenance, purchasing, and etceteras. At the time, I didn't give him or the others more than a cursory check. Maybe I should have dug deeper.

Tiffany picked up her glass and took another long sip of water. As she drank, her eyes bored holes into me from over the rim. When she was done, she set it back down on the counter, gently this time. She smirked at me and remained mum, teasing me by not saying anymore. It was okay; it was the least I deserved.

We both knew that I would never hesitate to call on anyone else; hackers, burglars, strong-arms, to help me out. But I wouldn't ask for any help from my own girlfriend, even when it was obvious that I needed it. Thankfully, she didn't bring up the last time I told her stay out of my business. If she hadn't defied me then, I'd be feeding fish in the Pacific Ocean.

"Okay," I sighed, resigned. "What about Bennett?"

"He runs the whole thing."

"What whole thing?"

"Pathways. There's not a single decision that is made by Sommers, Belinda, or anyone else in there; he's it. They are all just his lackeys, especially Sommers."

"Do you think he's the one driving the extortion plot against God's Way?"

"I absolutely do," Tiffany said adamantly. "I'm telling you Jack; you don't have to be there very long to see who's pulling all of the strings in this puppet show."

"And those strings go right down to the window dressing, Sommers and his wife?" I added.

"Exactly."

I looked out the big picture window that faced the ocean. It was only two o'clock in the afternoon but already the marine layer was coming in and making everything gray. I considered what Tiffany had just told me. There was no doubt that it was extremely valuable info, info that might have taken me too long to discover on my own. I had been focused too much on Sommers and his wife. I needed to change gears.

"Thanks Tiff," I said, turning back to her and smiling.

"You're welcome Jack."

She took her glass and put it into the dishwashing machine.

"So what's up with Belinda?" she asked over her shoulder. "Did your little 'honey trap' work?"

"Yeah," I said. "She wants to jump my bones to seal the deal."

"When?"

"Tomorrow."

Tiffany stepped slowly toward me, her lithe body nearly slinking as she walked. She put her arms around my neck and leaned in close to me. I wrapped my arms around her back.

She brought her mouth close to mine and breathed, "And are you going to let her jump your bones, Jack?"

I let my hands slowly move down over the small of her back and to her behind. I gripped the cheeks and pulled her toward me, her pelvis yielding easily.

"No," I said, just before we kissed. "Not her, but someone else."

NINETEEN

Belinda Sommers was a fashionably late to our little rendezvous. Like with Mentzer, and probably several others, she had setup the tryst at the Starlite Motel. Fine by me. I got there early and had the room rented and the cardkey in my hot little hand. Also, quite possibly like Mentzer and the others, I was told to wait in the car for her to show up.

In addition to these specific instructions, she also warned me that she would be coming in disguise lest one of Pathways' congregates spied her pulling into the lot and wondered just what was going on with the minister's wife. She reassured me and told me not to worry though, as underneath her costume it would be *all her*.

Again, I assured her that this was fine. As much as possible, I wanted her to stick with her proven plan and to be lulled into a sense of comfort. The fewer red flags I raised, the better. For my part, I just had to play the part of the randy husband out catting around while his wife was away.

For the remainder of the previous day, I had embarked on a data-mining quest for information - good, bad, and ugly - on Pathways' Chief Operations Officer, Tim Bennett. And like many a California forty-niner, I went bust before too long.

Based upon Bennett's headshot, he appeared to be in his late forties to early fifties. He was white, pale, and had thin, brown hair that he kept combed over his smooth pate in a futile attempt to hide his baldness. His eyes were dark, tiny, and intense, and although he smiled for the picture, it was obvious that it was forced and not with the same natural ease that Sommers and his wife had.

His website fluff bio told me nothing other than what his sundry duties were at Pathways; *"working to ensure the smooth operation of an organization committed to glorifying God and spreading the word…blah, blah, blah."* They were indeed spreading something at Pathways, but it wasn't "the word."

I tried searching his name through the Emperium website, and found that I could only come up with historical information for the past several years, about the same amount of time he had been with Pathways. Before then, it was essentially blank. The one interesting tidbit I did uncover, was the fact that Bennett was currently training to be a helicopter pilot, and was busy racking up hours flying the church's leased Augusta A109.

A reverse picture search yielded no results either, and I guessed that he had either had extensive plastic surgery performed, or he had done a stellar job of cleaning up his persona from the web. Like everyone in the top strata of Pathways, they had all seemingly materialized from out of nowhere.

Through the Aston Martin's rearview mirror, I could see Belinda Sommers' Mercedes pull into the same spot she had on the day that Mentzer had taken the plunge. I was directly in front of her.

I watched as, once again, she pulled down the visor and made a big show of checking her makeup in the mirror. I wasn't sure, but it seemed that I could see a black speck on the visor that was probably the lens for the camera. As soon as she got out of her car and I saw her running lights flash, I climbed out of the Aston.

She stepped toward me and I gave her a leering look of approval for her outfit. It was the same suit, red wig, and hat she wore when she met with Mentzer, although she might have switched sunglasses.

"Nice," I said hungrily. "Can't wait to see what's underneath it all."

She licked her lips and this action put an even glossier sheen on her lipstick.

"You will," she assured me. "In just a little while, you'll be totally convinced that Pathways is the church for you."

"Then let's get started with Sunday School," I said, and gestured to our room.

We walked over to the room, I slid in the card-key, and the door lock clicked open. I pushed the lever down and held the door open for her. She stepped in and made a show of looking around like it was all new to her. I hung the "Do Not Disturb" sign on the outside handle, and closed the door.

Belinda tossed her hat and her glasses onto the bed, but left her wig on. She turned to me. I took her in my arms and said, "So then Red, where do we begin?"

She leaned up closer to my face, pursed her full lips, but then held off from kissing me. She squinted her green eyes to try to make it look like her olfactory sense was being brutally offended.

"Ohhh," she said, recoiling. "You're going to have to clean up a little bit."

"Clean up?" I said innocently, and held up one of my arms to sniff at the pit.

"Oh," I said. "I guess you're right."

Banking on the fact that this may have been her ruse, I had purposely not bathed for a day or so. Tiffany hated it, but I told her it was for "the cause."

At the time, she had warned, "Well, it better not go on too long...be-*cause* you'll be looking for someone new to bump into during the night if you're going to continue to smell like the inside of a barn."

I assured her I would not.

Belinda smiled seductively at me to underscore the importance of my gaining some proper hygiene if we were going to play. "Besides," she purred. "I want to explore every inch of you, and I can't do that if you're stinky."

"Mmmmm. I see your point. I'll be right back...squeaky clean."

I winked my eye, uncoupled from her, and headed to the bathroom. I closed the door and turned on the shower. Then I stood by for about thirty seconds before opening the door and stepping back out into the room.

Belinda was at the door to our room, frantically pushing down on the lever and trying to open it. She was wasting her time; I had modified the mechanism so that only I could open it.

"Going so soon?" I asked.

TWENTY

"I…I just left something in my car," she stammered. "I just… What's wrong with the door? I can't open it!"

I stepped further into the room, deliberately taking my sweet time. She had picked up her hat and sunglasses from the bed and in their place, had left a note folded in half. I picked it up.

She watched me pick it up and she jiggled the door handle even more violently. Nothing was happening, so in desperation, she kicked at the bottom of the door with the toe of one of her designer shoes, scuffing the tip of it in the process.

"Forget it, Belinda," I said nonchalantly. "I modified the door. It won't open unless I want it to."

She looked at me, panicked. Gone from her face was the sultry smile and the air of smug confidence.

"I'll scream!" she warned. "I'll scream and the people in the next room will hear me. And…and the police will come and you'll be arrested. I'll say you kidnapped and raped me!"

"Nice try," I said. "But besides this room, I rented the ones on either side and above us; no one will hear you if you scream. Go ahead and try it if you want to waste your breath though."

I unfolded the note and read it.

It said: *We have video of you going into the motel room with another woman. We are going to show it to your wife if you don't cooperate with us.*

I held up the note in front of me. "But I guess if the police did come, I could always show them this little blackmail note that you left."

Her face fell and she was panting as heavily as if she had just run the 100-yard dash.

"Video," she managed to choke out in desperation. "We have video of you and I coming in here. Your wife is going to see it. Even if the police arrest me, we'll find a way to get it to her. Your only choice is to cooperate with us. You'll be ruined and lose all of your money - or rather, your wife's money - if you don't go along with us!"

"Video?" I said. "What video, Belinda? If that's even your real name. You mean the one that you took from the visor cam in your car? That video? The same type of video that you took of Mentzer before you drove him to suicide."

The last statement hit a nerve. At least I knew that she was, in fact, human.

"Shut up!" she screamed, covering her ears. "I didn't drive him to suicide! He just couldn't live with himself because he cheated on his wife."

I shoved the blackmail note in my pocket and continued stepping slowly toward her.

"He didn't cheat on his wife, Belinda," I fired back. "Because he couldn't have even gotten his pants down in the amount of time you two were in this room. He may have had intent, but he never did the deed because you were out of here in a flash before anything could happen. Probably used the same 'you need a shower' line on him."

I tapped my hand on the pocket where I had filed away the note. "Maybe even the same note?" I suggested.

"You…you don't know that!" she protested. "You don't know anything!"

I moved around the end of the bed and started slowly closing in on her.

"Sure," I admitted. "I don't know everything Belinda, but I know an awful lot. I know that I happened to be here on the same day that you and Pastor Roy came into this very room, and that - like you - I took some video of my own. I saw the whole thing go down Belinda"

Her face looked even more terrified. She was getting pale. Sweat was starting to come from under her red wig and bead up on her forehead. I continued on, unperturbed and bereft of any sympathy for her.

"And I know that you took video as well. And that you, and your scumbag husband, and Bennett are using videos to try to blackmail people for money - or for their entire churches."

She couldn't face me and looked down to the floor in shame. Her hands went up to cover her ears again.

"Shut up!" she screamed.

"And I know about the little visor camera in your car Belinda, the one that you think captured video of you and I coming into this room. Look out the window for your Benz Belinda; see if you can find it."

Hesitantly, she leaned away from the door and pulled back the thick curtain that covered the window. Her hands were visibly shaking. She craned to look out the window, her head swiveling around desperately as she tried to spot her car.

"It's already gone, Belinda," I said, continuing my slow march toward her. "It's gone and so is the memory card to your camera."

She let go of the curtain and moved over into the closest corner she could find to cower in. I kept moving toward her.

"Don't hurt me," she pleaded.

"I'm not going to hurt you," I said.

"Then, what do you want?" she asked timidly. "I'll do anything you want. Any kind of kinky sex, I'll do it. Just get my car back and let me go. I swear we won't tell your wife about this."

"I'm not even married," I said, then added, "and my name's not Donaldson."

I was just a foot or so away from her. In her face, I could see that all of the confidence was gone, the steely resolve. She had thought she was holding all of the cards and now realized that she had nothing. All the fight in her had vanished.

"What…what do you want?" she sobbed.

"The truth Belinda," I said, "About you, about Sommers, Bennett, about Pathways and all of its wicked schemes. That's all I want."

Her hands came up suddenly and she lunged toward me. I thought she was going on the attack and I prepared myself for it. But instead of screaming, biting, and clawing, she buried her head into my chest and began wailing uncontrollably.

"Save me!" she cried.

TWENTY-ONE

I'll have to admit, I held onto her for a long time, feeling a bit of guilt for causing her to break down. But after a little while, I reminded myself not to fall prey to sympathy; she was a part of the Pathways blackmailing juggernaut, and was complicit in the machinations along with Sommers and Bennett.

"Save you from who?" I asked when she had calmed down a bit. "Your husband or Bennett?"

She shook her head. "Not Ronald, he's stuck just like me. Bennett is the one who put it all together and he pulls all of the strings."

"And what did he put together?"

"The plan to have me seduce some of our congregates so we could blackmail them into tithing more money."

I nodded that I understood, but I wanted her to keep expounding, and to do that I had to make her more comfortable. I set her down on the bed and went into the bathroom, returning in a few moments with a piece of tissue. She took it, wiped her eyes and then blew her nose, ever so daintily. I'm sure a butterfly's sneeze was more violent.

"What about extorting the churches, like God's Way?"

She exhaled a huge sigh, like it felt good for her to confess. "Bennett got tired of just 'picking up the crumbs' as he would say. So he graduated to targeting entire churches instead of just getting a little bit here or there with wealthy patrons. He's crazy, and he's controlling us."

"How is he controlling you?" I asked. "What does he have on you, Belinda? And is that your real name?"

She thought about it for a long time before answering, considering how much to tell me. But then, reason won out over fear, and she came to the sad conclusion that she didn't have much choice in the matter. She was trapped in a hotel room with a man who had evidence that she was attempting to blackmail him, and who seemed to know a lot more about her than she knew of him.

"No," she said finally. "It's Sara, Sara Kelly." She said it like it had been a long time since she had heard herself say her own name.

"What about you?" she asked, turning toward me. "What's your name?"

"Jack," I said. "Just Jack."

Now that the introductions were complete, I steered her back to the topic at hand.

"Okay Sarah," I said, finding it surprisingly easy to start calling her by a different name. "How is Bennett controlling you? What the hell do you have in your past that he's using on you?"

"How do you know he has something on me?" she asked.

"Because I know that's how these things work. I know that he would have to have some leverage on you to be able to control you this way." Then I added, just to get a reaction out of her. "If what you're telling me is true."

She stiffened and the bed shook a little.

"I am telling you the truth!" she swore. "I am!"

We both heard a noise then; it was her phone vibrating in her purse. She pulled it out and looked at the display. She sighed wearily.

"Speak of The Devil," she said. "It's Bennett." She touched the "ignore call" key on the display screen and dropped it back into her purse.

"So what is it Sara? What does Bennett have on you from your past?"

She looked down at her feet, and turned her foot to examine the scuff mark on the toe of her shoe. She had really screwed it up and would have to toss the pair.

"I was with a guy once," she began slowly. "We were living in the midwest, Missouri actually. My boyfriend wasn't exactly what you'd call a boy scout. He'd do petty theft, sell a few drugs, and we somehow got by with it all. Then one day, he went too far and got into a big beef with another guy - I don't even remember what it was about. A gun went off during the argument, and the guy ended up dying. My boyfriend got arrested for murder and so did I, as an accessory."

Her attention left her shoes and she looked up to me with a pained expression on her face.

"I didn't do anything," she said emphatically. "I swear it. I hated confrontation and was in the other room. But you know how it is if you're just a lowlife loser with nothing more than a pathetic public defender to try to save your ass; they stuck me with it."

"And you couldn't beat the charge at all?"

"No. They reduced it some, but I was still sent to prison for four years. Chillicothe, Missouri. I was so scared and I feared for my life constantly. Then one day, I saw a chance to escape and so I did."

I nodded; it all was coming together.

"So you're a fugitive?" I said.

"Yes," she said in a voice that was barely above a whisper.

"How long?"

"Six years," she said. "Six *long* years of looking over my shoulder, always waiting for the other shoe to drop."

"How did you survive on the run?"

"First, I got as far away from there as I could. And then, like a lot of women's fallback plans, I sold myself. Not streetwalking mind you, high-class escort service stuff. That's where Bennett found me. He dug into my past and when he realized what I had done, he had me over a barrel. I was doomed. He protects me and keeps me hidden nicely, so I'm safe for the time being. But he'd dime me out in a heartbeat if I didn't play along with his scheme."

"You're the proverbial bird in a gilded cage," I offered.

She nodded sadly.

"What about Ronald?" I asked. "Is he really your husband?"

"No," she answered simply.

"What's his background then?" I followed up, since she wasn't going to elaborate.

"I don't know," she said. "But I'm sure Bennett has something on him as well. We pretty much stay out of each other's business - and Bennett keeps it that way."

"Well, you sure are convincing as a couple," I observed.

"Thanks," she shrugged. "I guess. But not good enough to fool you."

"Not many people fool me," I said.

Just then, her phone went off again. She looked at it and hit "ignore" again.

"It's him again" Sara Kelly, aka Belinda Sommers said wearily. "I'm going to have to go pretty soon."

"All right, but we need to talk some more so you can fill me in on the rest of this. Where and when can we meet again?"

"I don't know," she shrugged. "Like I said, Bennett keeps close tabs on everyone, especially Ronald and me. He wants to know where we are at all times."

"What about meeting at Pathways for a "follow-up" meeting?" I suggested.

She shook her head. "No. Too many cameras and listening devices around."

I nodded that I understood the risks involved.

"I saw the cameras," I said.

"Those are just the ones Bennett *wants* you to see," she said.

"Paranoid huh?"

"Incredibly so."

I pondered our quandary. “So this is about the only chance you have to be away and on your own?” I asked.

“Pretty much.”

“Okay, then we’ll have to meet again, here.”

“But why meet again? Bennett will demand to know. By now, you would be in our pocket.”

I pulled out my phone, dialed, and sent a voice text.

“Corrupt the video card,” I spoke into the phone. “I repeat; corrupt the video card, then return the car to the motel.”

In a few seconds, a ping let me know that my message had been received. I looked at the display and read it.

“Five minutes,” I said, turning toward Sara.

“Why’d you do that?” she asked innocently. “Why’d you have them corrupt the card?”

“So we can meet again,” I said simply.

She looked at me puzzled.

“When you get back from these setups, Bennett has you turn over the video card to him so he can download it. Correct?”

“Yes.”

“Well I don’t want it to have any usable data on it. It’ll be corrupted. It happens to these memory cards from time to time so he shouldn’t be suspicious. That will give you an excuse to see me again so you can fill me in on the rest of what’s going on.”

She looked away from me and considered my plan, then she found a major wrinkle in it.

“But what about the fact that I would have run out on you after I left you the note? Even if the card was corrupted and we didn’t have any dirt on you, our plot would have been exposed to you by then. You would realize that you luckily dodged a bullet, and would never come anywhere near Pathways after that."

Whew! She was good at thinking things through; I'd give her that. I stood up and began to pace, pondering. After a few moments I spun back around toward her, snapping my fingers in the process.

"Okay," I said. "Here's the scenario… you dupe me into the shower and then drop the note and run back to your car. Before you take off though, you hit play to check the video and you see that it's useless. You realize then that you have to go through with it and come back into the room before I'm out of the shower."

"So then we would have really done it, right?"

"Right," I said triumphantly, but then I hit another snag.

"Except that may not work," I said.

"Why?"

"Because based on the fact that your phone has been going off, and from what you've told me about Bennett, he's going to get very nervous and will probably send somebody out to check on you, right?"

She nodded. "Right. They might be on their way now."

"Okay, so here's the rest of the story since you have to get back to him pretty soon; you came back into the room and realized you would have to go through with it, but I couldn't get it up. You assured me that it was just nerves and that we should try again. I promised to take Viagra next time so I could really sow my wild oats instead of having a crop failure."

She giggled. "That's funny," she said. "I never heard that one before."

"Old joke," I admitted.

She was quiet for a while and then it hit her that she was far from out of the woods.

"But what about me?" she said finally. "We meet again, and I help you by spilling the rest of the beans about Pathways, but where does that leave me, Jack? I may have helped you, and saved my skin in the short term, but at the end of the day, I'm still a fugitive on the run, and Bennett's going to rat me out big time. My problems are far from over, and I may be going from the frying pan to the fire."

"I can take care of it, Sara," I said. "I promise you. I know all of the right people. I'll get you out of this and safe from Bennett or any others."

She nodded slowly, wearily. Being a fugitive and having to always look over her shoulder had taken its toll. She looked like the last six years on the lam had all caught up to her in the past few minutes.

"I hope so," she said.

Her phone went off again for the third time. She gestured toward it with a trembling hand and then Sara Kelly, fugitive, seductress, and faux wife of the charismatic Pastor Ronald Sommers turned to me and said, "It's all smoke and mirrors, Jack. The whole damn thing is nothing but smoke and mirrors."

TWENTY-TWO

Since the deadline for God's Way to merge with Pathways was fast approaching, before we left the Starlite Motel, I convinced Sara to meet me the following day at eleven o'clock for our next make-believe tryst. She checked the schedule on her phone and told me she would have to move some appointments around, but that it would work and she'd see me then.

I pulled the Aston Martin into the lot of the Starlite Motel the next day at ten forty-five and was surprised to see that her Mercedes-Benz was already there and parked in its usual spot. Maybe Sara had been able to break free early and we could afford a little bit more time to talk.

Playing the same charade we had previously acted out, I pulled my car up in front of her car, right by the motel office. I pulled out my phone and called her cell to ask what room she was in.

Her phone rang and rang and then finally the call went to voicemail.

"It's me," I said when the beep to leave a message sounded. "Call me back and let me know what room you're in. I don't want to have to go all around banging on doors."

I terminated the call and waited. After a moment, my phone pinged that I had a text. It was from her.

The text read: *Rm 5*

I looked at the text and then at the door to room five. Something didn't feel right.

I replied to the text with my own. *Call me*, I typed in and then hit "send."

I waited.

After a few seconds, I caught some movement in the office window in front of me. It was my old friend and client Stan, the man who lived every waking moment of his life waiting for his wealthy grandmother to kick the proverbial bucket, the man whom I had thrown a wrench into the best-laid plans of.

I didn't like him and he didn't like me. But what I really didn't like was that he was staring out the window at me. And that today, he was smiling.

"Shit!"

I started the Aston just as two of the goons from Pathways burst out of the door to room five. They were making a beeline toward my car.

The car's big motor caught and roared to life. I threw the shift lever into reverse and peeled rubber out of the space, whipping the wheel and nearly hooking one of the Pathways' muscle-heads in the process.

I threw the shifter into drive just as out of the corner of my eye, I saw hands reaching into jackets and hardware coming out.

Just then, another car that was parked in the lot pulled lengthwise across the driveway to the Starlite, blocking my escape.

"Damn it!"

A man emerged from the blocking car and I saw him reaching for a shoulder holster under his jacket. Before long, it was going to turn into a reenactment of the shootout at the OK Corral!

I threw the Aston into reverse again, punched it, and whipped the wheel extremely hard. It was a driving maneuver known as a J-turn, but was often referred to as a *Rockford*, a handy evasive maneuver made famous by the James Garner TV series.

The move served to fishtail the front of the car back toward the first set of goons, but more importantly, lined up the rear of my car with the car blocking the driveway. The two goons had their pistols lined up on my windshield and were aiming at my head.

I put the Aston Martin into reverse again and stomped on the accelerator, unleashing all five hundred horsepower to the rear wheels.

I ducked down into the passenger seat just as the first of the bullets glanced off the sloped windshield, cracking it in the process.

The man in the blocking car had to dive out of the way as I rammed his car and sent it skidding out onto Pacific Coast Highway. It destroyed the rear end of my $200,000 sports car, but I saved the front radiator, and therefore my ass, in the process. Just like the most neophyte driver in the demolition derby soon learned: you needed a cooling system if you were going to keep on boogying.

Out on Pacific Coast Highway it sounded like the walls of Jericho coming down as a chorus of horns sounded in unison when the goon's car sailed out onto the street. I flipped the wheel around and shoved the Aston Martin into drive again.

My foot nailed the accelerator to the floor just as a round took out the passenger's side window. The bullet came through and hit the side of my headrest. It made a loud thumping sound, and foam shot out from the hole in the leather covering. So much for resale value.

I put a good distance between myself and the Pathways army, and then made a few quick turns to lose myself in the pricey wooded neighborhood of Lomita Pines. I pulled over on a quiet, treelined street and got out my phone.

"Dial Hassan Towing," I said.

The call was answered a few moments later and I asked to speak to the owner himself, Hassan.

I had recently discovered that after getting access to the AAA database of membership info, Hassan Towing was running a neat little scam by making phony calls for assistance. They had the cardholders' names, vehicle info, and most importantly, their cell phones numbers. They would spoof the cell number, make the bogus call to have their car towed or their battery jumped, and then back-charge the Auto Club for the service. Like every other scammer I knew, life was all roses for them until One Eyed Jack poked his nose into it.

The dispatcher said that the owner was busy at the moment, and asked if someone else could help me? I said, no, and then told the dispatcher to tell Hassan that it was Carl Cleaver on the phone and that he better talk to me now. I was put on hold for a few moments before Hassan came on.

"I'm not behind on my payments," was the first thing he said to me.

"I know," I said. "I need a flatbed tow truck and a car cover right now."

"I don't have any trucks avail - "

"Bullshit!" I screamed. "You won't have a fucking tricycle to tow your Radio Flyer wagon if I dump the goods about you to Triple A! Understand Hassan?"

He cursed under his breath and asked me where I was.

I looked at the address on the nearest house and gave it to him.

"Okay," He said. "Ten minutes."

"Five, or you're out of business," I said.

"Infidel!" he spat before hanging up.

As soon as the call cleared, I redialed.

"Starlite Motel," Stan's musical little voice announced when he answered.

"Destroy the security tapes right now before the cops get there or you will never see a dime of that old hag's inheritance. You got it?"

"Got it," he said sadly before I hung up on him.

* * *

Tiffany was in the bathroom and just switching off her blow dryer when I stepped in. She could see by the expression on my face that something was terribly amiss.

"What's wrong, Jack?"

"Where are you going?" I asked her impatiently.

"To Pathways for reher - "

"No, you're not," I told her emphatically.

She set the blow dryer on the counter and held her hands out, exasperated.

"Why? What's going on now?"

"Belinda, or rather, Sara, set me up."

"What! What happened? How do you know?"

"They tried to kill me."

"What! Who?"

"Pathways goons," I said. "Her car was in the parking lot of the Starlite before I got there. She, or they, tried to lure me into the room. When I didn't fall for it, they came out in full force."

Tiffany turned away silently and stared into the brightly-lit mirror. She drummed the perfectly-manicured nails of her right hand on the counter. She had that habit when she was either angry with me, or when she was in deep thought. I had enough battles for the day and hoped it was the latter. She turned back to me.

"I don't think so, Jack."

"What do you mean you don't think so? I was there! I saw her car!"

"I know that. I'm just not sure if it was Sara who double crossed you."

"Why?"

"Because she's gone."

TWENTY-THREE

"What do you mean, gone?" I asked.

"Just what I mean - gone," Tiffany replied as if we were playing a word game.

"How do you know?

"This morning, we were supposed to practice at ten, so I went in about nine-thirty."

I considered what she said for a moment.

"Right, I remember you leaving - "

"Yeah," I continued, switching gears. "Speaking of which; why are you going back again for rehearsal?"

"The bassist had a family emergency and called in," Tiffany explained. "We all talked about it and decided we would just rehearse this afternoon when he could make it."

"All right," I said. "That explains that. So how do you know that Sara is gone?

"Gwen, she's the flutist, she works in the church and she's, well - "

"A busybody and a gossip?"

"Yes."

"There's lots of those in God's house it seems," I said wryly. "But they're my kind of people…if you know what I mean."

"I'm sure they are," Tiffany said sardonically. "Anyway, she was the one who told me."

"When was this?"

"Pretty much as soon as I got there at nine-thirty. I'm sure she couldn't wait to tell someone. But it happened yesterday."

"Yesterday?"

"Yes. I guess there was some big kind of a hub-bub yesterday when Sara got back to the church."

"Ostensibly after seducing me," I offered.

"Right." Tiffany arched a warning eyebrow at me.

"Okay. Go on," I said maybe a little bit too impatiently.

"So after this big brew ha-ha, Sara supposedly got marching orders to go overseas to one of the church's missions to help out with some emergency. It was a big rush and her calendar was cleared of all of her appointments. I guess they are going to announce it that she is over there at the next service on Sunday."

I paced around, as much as you can pace in a bathroom, and ended up sitting down on the end of a two-person Jacuzzi tub we had installed recently. My head dropped into my hands and I rubbed my face. For what was supposed to be a simple case of infidelity, this thing had morphed into a giant monster I barely recognized, and one that I was finding harder and harder to slay. It almost made me want to pull the plug, throw out all the dirt I had on everybody, and let the chips fall where they may. But I was never a quitter and wouldn't start now. I would be throwing Roy Mentzers family, God's Way Church, and now Sara - if she indeed hadn't betrayed me - under the bus. How the hell did I become responsible for everyone else's happiness?

"I don't think she's gone," I said finally, talking through my hands.

"You don't?"

"No. At least not the way they say she is. I don't buy this overseas mission crisis bullshit. Although, they could have sent her away to silence her."

"What do you mean silence her? Do you think they suspect that the two of you talked?"

I dropped my hands and looked up at Tiffany.

"No," I said. "I don't think they suspect, Tiffany. I think they know."

"How?"

I thought about the claim I was making and how it could play out.

"A couple of ways," I said. "One, Bennett could have not believed her story when she got back and put her feet to the fire until she cracked and told him the story about what really went down."

Tiffany's face twisted up in an expression of skepticism. "I don't know, Jack. She's a pretty good performer if she can pull off this nicey-nice role when she's really a snake in the grass."

"I agree," I said. "She's good. But remember, the worst person to try to bullshit is another bullshitter, and Bennett's probably the king of them all."

Tiffany hesitantly nodded that she was sold on the concept, but then I found myself doubting my own words. I thought back to Sara's phone vibrating incessantly while we were talking at the motel. It was like Bennett knew what was going on and he wanted to put a sock in her mouth.

"But that's not it," I said confidently.

"It's not?"

"No. She was bugged."

"Really? They would do that to one of their own?"

"I have no doubt. She verified that Pathways - or rather Bennett - is extremely paranoid, and that they have security cameras and listening devices everywhere. They could have easily had a bug in her purse, or even her cell phone could have been compromised to broadcast even when she wasn't making a call. I've done it myself numerous times."

Tiffany nodded her head that she understood. Then she looked up at me with a sense of dread on her face.

"Jack, if you're right and they were listening to her confessing to you about what was going on, could they have…?"

"Yeah," I said, finishing the horrible thought. "They could have silenced her permanently."

"But how would they explain it when she didn't come back to Pathways? At a certain point, people would begin to wonder."

"Easy," I said. "Look at where all of Pathways' missions are; dangerous, primitive, third-world countries. They could say that she was killed in a car crash, or by rebels, she could have been kidnapped. Hell, those parts of the world are like powder kegs. And with incompetent police departments and corrupt governments that could be bought off to look the other way when someone supposedly disappears - who's to say otherwise?"

We both were silent for a long time, letting the gravity of the possibilities sink in. Finally, Tiffany broke the quiet.

"I'm going to rehearsal, Jack," she said.

"No, you're no - " I started to say.

"Damn it Jack!" she yelled. "You need me now more than ever! You and I have no connection as far as they know, so there's no risk to me. But you, based on what you just told me, are now persona non grata there, and you won't be able to get within a hundred feet of the place. I'm your only source of intel from this point on. Plus, if all of a sudden I stop showing up right after this happened to you, then they would put two and two together. And unlike you, I'm in completely above board with no phony identity. If I don't return to Pathways and act like nothing is going on, they'll start trying to track me down to get to you. Do you want that?"

I shook my head.

"No," I said. "Just be careful, okay?"

"I will Jack."

"And don't act too interested in what's going on around there. Just let the blabbermouths come to you."

She walked over to the tub and reached down for me to stand. I stood up and we embraced and kissed yearningly for few moments.

"I've got to call Zahid," I said, breaking free.

"Why?" Tiffany asked. "I thought you told me he had reached a dead end with this and couldn't get through the church's firewalls?"

"He has reached a dead end," I said. "I'm going to help him bust through those firewalls. And I can do it if he can get me something else."

"What's that?"

"All the information on Pathways' security system," I said.

"Why?" Tiffany asked suspiciously, her voice sounding like she really didn't want to hear the answer - which she was correct in assuming.

"Because I'm going in," I said.

TWENTY-FOUR

"What the hell do you mean, you're afraid of heights?" I bellowed.

"Terrified of them. I always have been, ever since I was a kid."

"But you're a second-story man," I protested.

"Not in the true definition of the word," he said. "I always took the stairs or rode up in an elevator. I wasn't one of these crazy guys you see in the movies, climbing up the side of a building!"

His name was Bill Scanlon, a career burglar, alarm systems wizard, and someone with whom I had a very unique relationship. After all, I nearly killed him once.

Several years prior, I had come home from a very dangerous case, only to find him inside my condo with my alarm disabled. A cable ran from a port on the alarm master panel to his laptop, confirming to me that he was no ordinary thief. Thankfully, I happened to have my suppressed Glock on me, and I drew it on him.

He froze, naturally thinking that he was smoked and that I was going to end his career or his life, right there and then. Instead, I just told him to sit down.

"I want to know everything about alarm systems," I said. "Including, and especially, my own."

We talked, and for the next two hours I learned more about security systems than I could have hoped to in a lifetime. At the end of our discussion, I demanded to see his ID, which as I figured he was smart enough not to carry.

Left with no choice but to interrogate him to find out who he was, I went to the Emperium website and began to pepper him with questions: name, address, social security number, birthplace, places he had lived, where he went to school, his sibling's names, his mother's maiden name, all the stats. And when we had gone through the questions once, I asked them all over again.

He answered every question correctly and was either the best I'd ever seen at assuming another person's identity, or he was who he said he was. I saved the data on him and told him then that I would let him go, and that I wouldn't snitch him out, if he agreed to work with me occasionally. He readily agreed, and I'd called on his services many times over the years. This was the first time he'd ever let me down, for of all things, acrophobia.

"But I can guide you," he said. "Do you have a body cam or something that can stream video through your phone?"

"Several."

"Good. Then we can do this," he promised.

I gave him all the info on the Pathways security system. Although I hadn't been able to roam around the facility and check out the equipment for myself, Zahid had been able to do the next best thing - he was able to find the records for the purchase orders for the equipment and the installation. Armed with this information, I now knew exactly what I was going up against.

Before Scanlon gave me the quick breakdown on what I was going to have to do to disable the alarm, he asked an obvious question.

"Do you care about them knowing you hit them, or are you going ghost?"

"Poltergeist all the way…they can't have any clue that I was there," I said.

The master burglar considered my answer carefully. If anyone would know how to get in and out like a phantom, it was him. Known as "The Fox," he was renowned for his ability to get into places, take what he wanted, and then getting out without leaving a trace. It was a dramatic departure from the average smash-and-grab burglar, and Scanlon's victims sometimes didn't know they had been broken into for days, or even weeks, later. They either thought they had misplaced their items or that someone known to them had taken them. Hitting a residence that had children or other relatives with substance abuse issues offered an even easier solution, as they were typically the primary suspects.

By the time the victims knew they had been robbed, dozens of other people had either contaminated the crime scene with their own biological markers, or they even cleaned up behind him.

"And you said that they have security cameras?" he asked rhetorically.

"Yes."

"That's a problem if you're going ghost," he said. "If someone reviews the recordings on a daily basis, or if they just have the slightest inkling that someone has broken in and they look at them, you're toast."

"Not if I shut off the power to them," I said. "There's no UPS, or battery backups for the camera, only the internal battery for the alarm master panel, right? No power equals no video."

"Right. But if you kill the power to the building by shutting off the breaker, they'll still know you were in, even if you turn it back on when you leave. Everything, computers and the cameras will have to be rebooted. That's going to raise red flags. They might think it was a localized power failure, but if they check with the utility company - "

"The utility company will tell them it was a real power failure," I said.

"Why would they do that?"

"Because I'm going to cause one," I said.

TWENTY-FIVE

The Bell 205 helicopter swept in above the expansive Pathways Church at 500 feet above the ground. All exterior running lights were switched off in the aircraft, and the interior instruments were muted a dull red. Originally developed as a civilian version of the UH-1 or "Huey," the aircraft made famous for its use in the Vietnam War, the Bell 205 was a versatile flying machine and could be configured for all kinds of civilian missions, including crop dusting, fire-fighting, and most importantly, rescue that required fast ingress into locations.

It was just past three a.m. and the streets were quiet at this hour of the morning. By now, all the drunks were either passed out at home, or at the police station being booked for DUI. This was also the time nighttime shift workers referred to as "the witching hour." It was the time when mistakes were made, and bad things would happen. And in just a few minutes, bad things were going to happen.

"How steady can you hold this thing?" I asked the pilot. "I don't want to miss my shot."

"Winds are fine," he said easily. "I can hold it rock steady as long as you need me to."

His name was Ryan Andrews, US Army retired, and he had extensive experience flying Blackhawk helicopters in Afghanistan until he was shot down during a combat mission. He had to evade capture from the Taliban for five long days until a SEAL team located and then rescued him. The experience left him scarred physically (he had lost several of the fingers on his left hand and had to have his shoulder rebuilt), but he wasn't damaged as much psychologically as he would have liked people to believe.

One of the people he needed to convince was a psychologist who contracted to the VA to analyze patients to determine if they were suffering from PTSD, and therefore qualified for lifetime disability payments.

Rather than take his chances at faking his way through the evaluation, Andrews decided to be proactive and do a little research into the affliction and how to answer some of the psychologist's probing questions about movie selections, or Fourth of July celebrations.

I caught wind of the scam when another psychologist, who I was leaning on for having an affair with his receptionist, coughed up to me how he had helped the former helicopter pilot secure his perpetual benefits by schooling him on the correct answers. FYI: Anyone with legitimate PTSD would not go to the theater to watch *American Sniper*.

"Thanks," I said. "Just hold it right here."

"You don't want it any lower?" Andrews asked. "To make your shot easier?"

"No. I need to maintain a downward trajectory. Just let me take my shot first, and then start slowly hovering down. When the real fireworks start, drop down real fast to about fifty feet off the deck."

"Got it."

I moved back from my seat in the cockpit, to the main cabin area, which had been stripped of its seats so that it was one big open deck. I pulled up on the handle of the side door and it slid open on its roller bearings effortlessly. Instantly, the cabin was filled with the deafening sound of the rotor wash and the thousand-horsepower turbine engine.

I grabbed an M25 sniper rifle out of its case and took up a prone shooting position on the deck of the 205.

Pathways was a big church, and one that required a lot of power. To meet the hefty demand, a large cylindrical oil-filled transformer was mounted high on a pole just adjacent to the church's property. The transformer basically reduced, or stepped-down, the line voltage of 4800 volts to a more sedate 480 volts before feeding it into the main breaker panels of the facility.

I wrapped the sling of the rifle around my wrist and back again to the opposite side of my biceps to "lock in" the weapon to my body and stabilize it. The M25 was equipped with a special low-light scope that automatically adjusted the brightness of the crosshairs so the shooter could see them even in the dead of night.

I pulled the rifle up closer to my face and repositioned it so that the crosshairs were directly on the center of the transformer can, and just a few inches from the bottom. I noted that the crosshairs barely moved about while I held it on the target; Andrews was just as good of a pilot as he claimed. I had a great shot. I switched off the safety and fired.

Like many cities, Los Angeles was no stranger to gunfire. In the inner cities of Compton, Watts, and South LA, several miles to the east of us, this was normally the result of drive-by shootings when turf wars erupted between rival gangs. But occasionally, weapons were discharged in the pricey beach communities of the South Bay as well. These occasional illegal discharges weren't generally violent in nature, and were typically the result of more jubilant motives.

As much as the police and fire departments cautioned against it every year, revelers - often inebriated beyond any sense of reasoning - loved to celebrate our nation's birth or to ring in the New Year by firing their guns into the air. No one engaged in these ad hoc displays of patriotism or conviviality ever thought far enough along to remember the old adage that, *what goes up, must come down.*

The falling projectiles would take out an occasional car windshield, hit a house, or depending on the direction, might harmlessly fall into the Pacific Ocean. And although it wasn't the Fourth of July or New Year's eve, many a wild bachelor party or birthday celebration had spawned similar displays of reckless merrymaking.

As soon as I fired the shot and recovered from the recoil, I reacquired the target to check it. It was a direct hit, exactly where I had aimed. Based upon our angle, and the downward trajectory of the bullet, it would look, to anyone who took the time to examine it, like one more idiot had thoughtlessly fired his gun into the air and inadvertently hit something. Through the scope, I could see transformer oil begin to flow out of the hole made by the metal-jacketed round. I turned toward the pilot.

"Get right over the atrium in the middle of the building and then bring us down slowly to about 200 feet!" I yelled.

"Got it," he said, and pushed on the helicopter's cyclic lever. The Bell 205 rolled slightly, then slid gently sideways over the target. In a moment we were hovering directly above Pathways' outdoor atrium. Andrews then readjusted the collective controls so that the pitch of the rotor blades decreased, and our lift diminished. In just a few seconds, we began to slowly descend.

In the meantime, I stowed the M25 and began getting ready for my insertion, which could come at any moment.

Electrical transformer oil is used for insulating, and to cool the internal coils and keep transformers from overheating. With no oil to cool them, the wires on the coils rapidly heat up and begin to fuse together, which causes greater current flow and even more heat. This triggers a cascade effect, and in short order, the coils reach a critical mass and the transformer explodes. How long that would take, and when it would happen, was the big question mark.

A nylon rappelling rope ran through a carabiner mounted to the middle of the cabin floor and then was tied off to an anchor between the front seats. I looped the rest of the rope through a figure-8 rappelling device connected to my climbing harness and hoisted a small pack onto my back.

"Altitude?" I called out.

"Three-hundred feet."

As we continued to descend, I tossed the rest of the rope through the helicopter door opening and watched it as it disappeared into the darkness. Below us, I could see the Pathways Church building, its exterior bathed in tall lights. I set my hands on the climbing rope in the classic rappelling hand placement; left hand above the device, right hand below with the rope, and against my hip.

We stopped descending and I heard Andrews call out our altitude.

"Two-hundred feet and holding."

"Okay," I said. "When it blows, I need you to get to fifty feet ASAP!"

"Roger."

I took up the slack of the rope until it was tense and began walking slowly backward out of the main cabin of the helicopter. I reached the edge of the open door, and using my right hand to throttle the tension, slowly fed the rope through its circuitous route of the figure-8 device until I was leaning backward at a forty-five degree angle out the door.

Feeling with one foot at a time, I located the Bell's landing skid and slowly stepped down onto it. The wash from the main rotor was like a hurricane out there and it was all I could do to keep from having it force me off the skids.

BOOM!

I looked behind me to see the transformer explode in a blinding flash! Burning insulating oil sprayed out and bathed the top of the wooden pole, igniting it. I looked away from the fire long enough to see the bright pole lights that illuminated Pathways go dark. Several office windows, which had, until just a few seconds ago, been illuminated by interior lights, extinguished as well. Thankfully, I had shot out the right transformer. The building was dead, and would stay that way until the electrical crews working through the night and the next day, repaired the damage caused by some gun blasting knucklehead.

"Get down now!" I yelled above the deafening rotor blast.

I felt my stomach go up into my throat, and my body go nearly weightless as Ryan Andrews dropped us down to fifty feet in a matter of seconds.

"Fifty feet!" he screamed out.

Then I released the tension on the climbing rope, stepped off the helicopter skid, and dropped into the dark abyss.

TWENTY-SIX

I felt the tops of the tall queen palms first as my boots made contact with the upper fronds. I kicked over, slowed my descent to a crawl, and lowered myself the rest of the way into the middle of the atrium. The leaves of several plants were brushing up against my face, making tiny cuts on my cheeks and chin. That was okay, at least I wasn't dropping down into the garden's waterfall.

As soon as my feet made solid contact, I pulled the remaining length of rope through the figure-8, and then dropped it on the ground. I pulled out a flashlight, aimed it up to Andrews in the Bell, and switched it on to "pulse." I gave him a couple of flashes and soon I heard the throb of the rotor blades change pitch as he climbed rapidly straight upward, the tag end of my climbing rope following him into the dark sky.

When he was about 300 feet off the deck, he turned and pitched the helicopter forward, heading back to the flight center where we had rented it earlier in the day. Then he disappeared from my sight, and I was on my own.

I took a quick look around and got my bearings. Tiffany had been given a cursory tour of the facility when she signed on to be their vocalist, and she had drawn a map for me based on her memory. My ultimate objective was to get into Bennett's office and to compromise his computer. But first I had to disable the alarm system and the shortest route to get there was through Sommers' office. I made a quick note to myself to be careful not to break any of the stalks or branches of the plants around me, lest I give an indication that I had been there.

I gingerly stepped out of the foliage and onto the crushed seashell path that bordered the garden. I scraped my boots onto the edges of a flagstone to remove any dirt from my boots, and then brushed it into the seashells.

At the sliding glass door that led into Sommers' office, I pulled off my pack and set it down on the outside patio. Then I stripped out of my climbing harness and stowed it in the pack, before extracting several other pieces of equipment that I would be using: a lock-picking gun or "snap-gun," a "Toughbook" laptop computer with alarm-programming software, a police scanner with earbud, a headset equipped with a laryngophone for stealth audio broadcasting, and most importantly, night vision goggles (NVG), that simulcast a real-time video stream.

I switched on the laptop so it would begin to boot up, and then switched on the police scanner and put the earbud into my left ear. Before long, 911 would be getting a call about the explosion and burning pole, and I wanted to keep tabs on the first responder situation.

Before putting on any other equipment, I sat down on the patio and unzipped my combat boots. I didn't want to leave any footprints or impressions on the carpet from the Vibram lug soles, and so I pulled off the boots and stowed them in my pack. Underneath, I had on a pair of hospital socks with rubberized grips that would allow me to pad around the hallowed halls of Pathways with low impact footwear.

Before long, I had mounted all the rest of my gear, and looked like a cross between *RoboCop* and a one-man band.

Through the throat mic I whispered, "Scanlon, are you reading me?"

"Loud and clear," came the response in my right ear.

From the earbud in my left ear I heard, "South Bay dispatch to any available units in the area of the Pathways Church. Reports of a loud explosion and possible fire."

A unit responded moments later.

"Roger South Bay, Lincoln-four from Sepulveda and Western."

Okay. So they were on their way and would arrive in a few minutes. I turned my attention back to my partner in crime.

"Switching on NVG Scanlon; tell me when you see video."

"Got it."

I activated the NVG and instantly the image to my eye changed from one of dark colorless shadows, to a milky green that was nearly as bright as day.

"Got it. Looks good. You've got a great camera setup. I'll have to get one."

I let it pass. I wasn't in the mood for chitchat. It had been a long time since I had done a B&E and I was nervous; a trickle of sweat snaked its way down my backside and I could hear my own labored breathing in the earpiece.

From my left earpiece again: "Lincoln-four to South Bay dispatch. On scene at Pathways. We've got a fire on the upper end of a power pole. Looks like the transformer blew."

"Roger Lincoln-four. RP said they heard a loud explosion before they saw the pole catch on fire. Torrance Fire is en route."

"Roger South Bay. Standing by for Torrance Fire."

In the distance, I could hear a fire truck's siren as it drove to the scene. I knew enough about fire fighting to know that they wouldn't try to extinguish the flames on an electrical fire if there were no other structures at risk, and would simply isolate the scene and deny entry until Edison Electric arrived. Good, they wouldn't pay any attention to the church.

"Okay," I said to Scanlon. "It's getting busy around here. I better go in now while they're all distracted."

"Copy that, Jack."

With just a tension wrench and a couple of snaps from the lock-picking gun, I was inside Sommers' office in seconds. Even through the heavy door to his office, I could hear the screech of the tiny local alarm built into the security systems' master control panel, letting me know that it had just registered a zone violation.

I knew that a silent alarm had already been sent to the alarm monitoring service when I killed the power to the building, and the unit had gone onto backup batteries. The alarm company probably would have to send a unit to the scene to check it out, but once they saw the pole on fire, and realized it was a genuine power outage, they would report the information back to the dispatch center. Whether or not they would do a cursory perimeter check, or contact the appropriate folks at Pathways, I couldn't say. But if I didn't get to the alarm panel and disable it before it timed out, they would get a general intrusion alarm and definitely investigate further. Already, the shriek was starting to sound like the desperate cry of a baby who needed attention.

I locked the outside door to the atrium and made quick tracks through Sommers' office. I stepped out into the hall and into the giant reception area, blocking the door open with a rubber doorstop as I moved through. If someone showed up and I had to fly on out of there, I didn't want to have to pick more locks on my way out.

I reached the master panel in the reception area and quickly went to work. It had a key lock on the front door of the panel that was cheap, and I was in it with the snap gun with one pull.

"Inside the box," I said to Scanlon. "Now what?"

"See the little jumper pin in the top left, about b-2 on the circuit board grid? It should have printing under it that says, *J-4*."

Through the green hue image of the NVG, I looked for the jumper pin Scanlon was talking about. It was tough to spot because the lights of the emergency vehicles outside would blind me through the goggle's display every time they flashed.

"Okay. I see it. Now what?"

"It should be set to the left side, and on pins zero and one."

I leaned in closer to see. God this was tough through the night vision goggles. I'd have given anything to be able to take them off and use a flashlight - or to have the incessant screeching sound go away. Finally…

"Yes," I confirmed. "On pins zero and one."

"Pull out the jumper and move it to the right so that it is on pins one and two."

I reached into the tiny box and wriggled the jumper loose. After I had it pulled, I reinserted in onto pins one and two. The alarm sound stopped. I breathed easier… a bit.

"Okay. On pins one and two," I said. "The alarm stopped. What next?"

"There's a switch in the upper right-hand corner. Turn it off, count to five, and then turn it back on again."

I did as I was told and I saw the front display on the panel go through a hard reboot.

"It looks like it's rebooting," I said.

"It is," Scanlon said. "You just bought yourself thirty uninterrupted minutes of maintenance time."

I looked down at my watch and made a note of the time: 3:17 a.m. I'd better be out by quarter to four.

"No zone alarm to the monitoring company?"

"No zone alarm."

I breathed out a sigh of relief.

"But remember," Scanlon warned. "We don't want to leave it this way, because the next time someone comes in, it won't audibly alarm while it's waiting for them to punch in the code and they'll get suspicious."

"So what do we do?" I asked. "Reset the jumper before we leave?"

"We could, but that's a pain in the ass. You're going to reprogram the unit so you don't have to come back out and do a reboot again. Connect your laptop to the port inside and launch the app I sent you."

I did as I was told, and over the next several minutes, Scanlon walked me through the necessary configuration screens. When I disconnected the cable, I asked him, "So what exactly did we do?"

"We reprogrammed the unit to give you an extra thirty minutes of maintenance time. So now you've got a little less than an hour left. I hope you work fast."

I checked my watch again, 3:32 a.m. Okay, I bought myself until four-seventeen, but that would be here before I knew it.

"I'll be out before four-ten. I guarantee it."

"Good. After the hour's up, the unit will do another hard boot and the new jumper setting will be, as we say "examined," and everything will seem normal to everyone. Unless someone goes through the program and the jumper settings, and notices the changes and compares them to the original configuration, they'll have no idea. Even then, they'll just chalk it up to some rookie technician who didn't know what the hell he was doing."

"Great Scanlon. Thanks."

"No worries. Just grateful I didn't have to come in the way you did."

We shared a laugh and he disconnected.

I closed the panel door and re-locked it using the snap gun. Then, I got ready to discover the deep, dark secrets of Pathways Church.

TWENTY-SEVEN

After pulling out the rubber doorstop, I bypassed Sommers' and Sara's offices, and headed straight to Bennett's. He was the dirtiest guy in the organization, and so that was where I would do my mining.

I quickly compromised the lock and stepped inside his office, or at least what I thought was his office.

Unlike Sommers' and Sara's offices, the head of operations for Pathways Church had the extra layer of protection afforded to him by having a receptionist office that isolated him from the main hallway. Inside, there were two small desks, each with a phone, several computer monitors, and not much else on them. There were some tall file cabinets set against the wall, as well as some bookcases. A few inspirational framed pictures were mounted on the open wall space above, but no family photos or anything else of a personal nature.

Several large-screen monitors flanked each side of the doorway I had entered through. All of the screens were dark. They were probably the display screens for the CCTV security system that I had buggered up with the power failure. The gatekeepers who manned this station were also probably not a couple of middle-aged women like the one at the main reception area, but rather, several of the thugs who had taken a shot at me the previous day. Bennett had a lot of protection, which meant he had a lot to hide. My kind of man.

I moved across the small office to another door and got through the lock in just a few seconds. I would have to remember to write a good review on Yelp for the manufacturers of the snap gun.

Bennett's office was slightly smaller than Sommers' or his faux wife's, and it was far less opulent. A simple medium-sized desk was situated in the middle of the room and had a multi-line phone, two computer monitors, a blotter, and a pen set on top of it. A couple of bookcases and cabinets were set against the walls, and there were some large framed photos of the Pathways' overseas missions mounted above them.

There was no conference table in the office, and only two chairs were set on the opposite side of the desk from Bennett's. It was obvious from looking at it that Bennett was a man who enjoyed his privacy and didn't hold with people invading his space.

I turned around and noted that, similar to the reception office outside, the same big-screen displays were mounted on the wall on either side of the door. Like the ones in the outer office, they were probably CCTV and were multiplexed to display up to a sixteen-channel grid on each screen. I considered myself lucky just to keep track of the two monitors on my home computer, let alone be able to watch all of this.

Bennett must have had as many eyes as a grasshopper.

I stepped around the far side of the desk, and before I did anything, made a mental note of how far the chair was pushed under the desk and at what angle. It was straight in, and the backrest was pushed all the way against the edge of the desk. Easy enough to reset when I was done.

I rolled the chair out far enough to give me plenty of room, and poked my head under the desk to take a look.

Crap! There were two computer towers and I had only one USB hacking device!

I stood looking at the towers and considering my dilemma for a moment until finally, resigned, I started to crawl under the desk. But then I paused and thought better of it. I pressed a button on the side of my NVG and heard an audible click, letting me know that I had taken a picture of the two towers and their respective locations. Bennett struck me as a guy who knew exactly where everything was and I couldn't count on him blaming the overnight cleaning crew - if there even was one, if something were amiss.

I dropped down to my belly and slid under the desk. The towers were separated from each other on either side of the underside of the desk. I looked at the back of the one to my left first and saw a hard network cable plugged into the port. Then I turned to the unit on my right - no network cable. Hmmm, that could only mean a couple of things.

One, it could have been linked by Wi-Fi to Pathways' intranet and/or outside Internet, but I didn't think that was very likely. I doubted that a guy like

Bennett would trust his dirty dealings to anything as vulnerable as a Wi-Fi connection.

The more likely scenario was that it was off the grid, both from Pathways' internal network, and the world's external one. This was known as "air-gapping," and was the computer world equivalent of abstinence. Air gapping was considered the only true way to insulate a device from Internet attacks.

I looked at my watch: 3:47 a.m. I didn't have oodles of time left before the security system would reboot and I would trigger the alarm on my way out. My whole stealth visit to Pathways would have been for naught. I stared at the isolated tower and knew that it probably contained the treasure I was hunting for.

Screw it.

I disconnected all of the cables on the air-gapped tower making a note of which port they went into and then pulled the unit out and onto the floor to open it. I removed the single Phillips-head screw and slid the chassis open to expose the internals.

Thankfully, I had only closed my laptop and had not powered it down. I flipped open the display, went to the main screen, and clicked on the "My Computer" icon.

I disconnected the ribbon cable that went to the tower's hard drive, and in its place, inserted another cable from one end of a hard drive converter I had brought along. The other end of the converter had a USB cable, and I plugged it into my laptop. In a few seconds, Bennett's computer hard drive showed up on my display as *Removable Disk (I:)*

In other words, it was now nothing more than an external hard drive someone would connect to their computer to backup their data. I double-clicked on the drive and navigated to his documents. Then I began a bulk copy of them to my laptop.

While the computer was copying all of the folders, I crawled back under Bennett's desk and examined the back of the other tower. There were three open USB ports and I installed a specially-designed device known as a "hacksaw," to the lowest open port.

Unlike most hacking devices, the hacksaw had been designed to be as unobtrusive as possible. Rather than protrude from the port and possibly attract attention, it was designed to fit flush, and was made of the same plated metal as the back plate of most computer towers. To the casual observer, it would only appear as if the computer had five USB ports instead of six. After all, do you remember how many USB ports your computer has?

The hacking device installed, I scooted back out on my knees to check the progress of the file transfer, and in the process raised up too soon, hitting my head on the underside of the desk.

Damn it! I cursed under my breath.

I rubbed my head and then checked for blood, of which there was none. Then I looked at the underside of the desk to see if I had left any hair follicles.

No traces of blood or hair were on the underside of the desk which was good, but there was a round circular device I recognized instantly as a gun magnet. The device functioned like an under-desk holster by using a strong magnet to hold stationary a sidearm of choice, but it was far less conspicuous.

Bennett was indeed a very paranoid person.

I stood up and rubbed my finger on the touchpad to awaken the laptop and check the file transfer progress.

Then I heard it.

TWENTY-EIGHT

It was a bumping sound, muted and emanating from somewhere inside the building. How close or far away, I couldn't tell.

I looked down at the copy files progress bar on the screen: about sixty percent. Sixty wasn't as good as one hundred, but it would be nothing if I got caught in here. Maybe the alarm company had been called. Or maybe the police had been allowed in to do a cursory check. Or maybe, worst of all, it was Bennett and his henchmen, not satisfied with the fact that it was a legitimate power outage.

I heard the sound again, which definitely sounded more like a thump than the sound of footsteps, talking, or doors being opened and closed. Still, it was getting dicey in there and I couldn't stick around.

I cancelled the rest of the file copy and as soon as I could, disconnected Bennett's hard drive from my computer. I reinstalled the original hard drive cable, and buttoned up the rest of it. I slid the tower back under his desk and reconnected all of the cables exactly as they had been.

Back out from under the desk, I took one last look at the layout and how I had left it. I decided it looked fine. I threw everything into my backpack, pushed Bennett's chair back into place, and then checked my watch: 4:03 a.m. I started making tracks.

* * *

Like any good criminal, I had figured out my escape route first, along with a backup. Rather than go out the way I had come in, through Sommers' office, or take a floor level exit, I turned right out of Bennett's office and down the main hall. At the end of the hall was a door to a stairway that led up the three flights to the roof access.

If anyone - police, Pathways' personnel, or someone else were going to check out the interior of the building to see if it had been infiltrated, they would naturally start at the ground level and work their way up.

Besides having the heliport, the roof also had an egress ladder that ran down the side of the building. Most people checking out a building for illegal entry might do a cursory perimeter search, but then the focus would shift inside to nab the bad guys. The good news for me was that if the thumping I heard was someone banging around on the inside of the building that meant that they had probably already cleared the outside.

I went up the two flights of stairs and got to the door that led out to the roof. The door opened outward and was locked from the outside, but not from inside, so that was fortuitous. But it was also fitted with a proximity switch to alarm it for unauthorized entry.

I checked my watch one last time and saw that I had only four minutes to spare before the alarm would reset. I breathed a sigh of relief, pushed on the door handle and stepped out on the roof.

The door was spring-loaded to close, but I didn't want to take any chances by being sloppy and made sure it was fully closed behind me, lest the alarm trigger when I was so close to getting away.

I didn't want to waste the time to put my boots back on, so I padded across the roof in my hospital socks. The roofing material was aggregate and the tiny rocks tortured my feet as I stepped on them.

I made it to the escape ladder, checked for any personnel, and finding none, was down the ladder and in my car in a matter of minutes. My mission was a success, somewhat.

* * *

As soon as I was out of harm's way, I realized that in addition to being soaked with sweat, I was starving to death.

Rather than head home and take a chance of waking up Tiffany by banging around in the kitchen, I stopped at The Kettle Restaurant on Manhattan Beach Boulevard. Besides offering great food at reasonable prices, The Kettle also served breakfast twenty-four hours a day, and was a great late-night spot for those craving a good omelet or some Eggs Benedict. Right now, some morning grub and strong coffee sounded like just what the doctor ordered.

I pulled into an empty parking space out front, changed out of my wet T-shirt, and went inside. Thinking I might be able to get a little work done and see what treasures I had commandeered from Pathways, I brought my laptop in with me.

The hostess told me to sit anywhere I liked, and I dragged up to a large booth by the widow and ordered coffee before she even had to ask. At this hour there were only a couple of working stiffs in here, as well as one guy who looked like he had dodged the DUI checkpoints and needed to sober up before he headed home to mamma.

I came here often enough to know the menu and asked for the breakfast burrito with a glass of orange juice. The waitress nodded and moved off, and I opened up my laptop and powered it up, navigating to the folder where I had copied Bennett's files.

My coffee arrived just seconds later and I took one sip before sloshing it over the rim of the cup.

"What the hell?" I said, louder than I had wanted to.

This caught my server's attention.

"Is everything all right?" she asked, genuinely concerned. "Is the coffee okay?"

"Yes," I stammered, embarrassed that I had caused her distress. "Everything is fine. Great, as a matter of fact."

I took another long slow sip and looked at the file I had opened, recalling the cryptic warning Sara had given me before she had mysteriously disappeared. Now I knew exactly what she meant by it.

TWENTY-NINE

"I…I'm sorry Jack. I just can't get used to it."

Tiffany made a face, and then stifled a giggle. My feelings weren't hurt, in fact, if she couldn't recognize me as the man she had been with for over half a year, probably no one else could either.

She had correctly stated that I couldn't get to within a hundred feet of Pathways without them spotting good old One Eyed Jack. Therefore, I had to become someone other than myself for the time being, and that required some radical changes.

My mustache and goatee were gone, as was most of my hair. I now sported a harsh crew cut that had been dyed blond. An extensive henna tattoo of the Madonna and a dying Jesus on the cross, covered a good portion of my neck, and three teardrops were on my right cheek, just under my eye, advertising to all of the world that I had done time.

More than anything else though, I went from being a Cyclops to someone who more closely resembled the other ninety-nine percent of humanity; I had inserted a glass eye into my empty socket and ditched the eye patch.

The fact that I had the prosthesis at all was in itself unique, something I had Dr. Karch and Viktor Durov to thank for. Not satisfied in having me merely lose half of my vision, the mobster also wanted me to be forever unable to blend in with the crowd. So in addition to removal of my eye, he instructed the good doctor to take it one step further by also removing the extraocular muscles that would allow me to properly wear a prosthesis. The end result of this was that I could wear a glass eye, but without the muscles to synchronize it with my remaining peeper. It would remain stationary instead of naturally following the other eye.

"I thought you said you couldn't wear a glass eye?" Tiffany asked.

"It doesn't look right, so I prefer the patch. But…"

I put on a pair of glasses with thick non-corrective lenses.

"…this should help."

"I would never recognize you," Tiffany said.

"Music to my ears."

My idiom jolted Tiffany back to reality. She glanced down to her watch.

"Oh, heck, speaking of music; I need to go."

Before she could start to move, I grabbed her.

"Remember what I said," I instructed. "After the first set of songs and Sommers takes the stage, you make a show that you have to go to the bathroom or something, and then just get the hell out of there."

She looked at me with a worried look. "All right, Jack," she said softly. "You be careful."

She took my face in both of her hands and kissed me gently. It felt wonderful.

"I will," I assured her. "See you in a bit."

She turned away and left. In a few moments, I heard her car start and pull out of the garage, before disappearing down the alley that ran behind our house.

With nothing more to do, I checked my phone and the program that Zahid had sent me. I went through the commands and rehearsed everything in my mind over and over for the umpteenth time. All the while I was thinking wryly that today's service at Pathways Church was going to be one that people would be talking about for a very long time.

* * *

I was surprised to see an extra long line of people at the main entrance to the church when I arrived a short time later. But as soon as I got out of my car and queued up behind the others that had made their weekly pilgrimage, I saw the reason why: security had been beefed up to the level of an airport.

Three lines had been formed and people were being subjected to having their purses and backpacks checked, as well as being forced to walk through a metal detector.

I had a short barreled Glock 9mm tucked into an inside waistband holster around my backside and I knew I'd never get through the security screening with it.

I made a sham of acting like I'd forgotten something in my car and returned to the parking structure to dump my hardware before I tried to gain access.

As soon as I got to the car though, I realized that I would feel naked going in without my weapon. I thought better of the plan to ditch it.

Instead, I compromised; I left the holster in the car, but tucked the pistol back into my waistband. I buttoned my suit coat over it and then headed back to the church entrance.

Rather than take up a place in the rapidly growing security line, I stepped inside the main foyer and turned right toward the men's bathroom. I entered the facility and was pleased to see that there was only one other man inside who was finishing up and washing his hands at the sink.

As soon as he was heading out, I went into the farthest handicapped stall, and with my right hand, closed and latched the door behind me. I retrieved the Glock from my waistband, and then listened to see if anyone else was coming in. When I didn't hear anyone, I quickly stepped up onto the toilet seat and pushed up a tile in the suspended ceiling. I stuffed the gun up onto an adjacent tile and reworked the open tile back into its place.

Just as I stepped down off the commode, my phone chimed that I had a text from Tiffany. It had a red exclamation mark, so I knew I'd better read it.

It read: *Just heard: Metal detectors at front entrance.*

I replied: *Got it handled. Thanks. Break a leg beautiful. XOXO*

Back in the security screening line, I overheard several comments by the other congregates while we were waiting, their remarks tending to be more speculative about the added security than irritability.

"...I wonder if it has to do with the fire the other night?"

"...you can't be too careful with all of the crazies in the world."

And...

"...Pastor Sommers knows what he's doing."

Not for long, I thought.

Inching forward with the masses toward the security checkpoint, I checked my phone now that I was closer to the entrance and saw that I was synched in to the necessary equipment. Perfect, that was going well. Now I just needed to get to the other side.

As more people went through, the handlers got more efficient and the line moved faster. I noted that several of the Pathways goons were standing off to the side and surveying the crowd, most likely on the lookout for a pesky one-eyed troublemaker. I recognized one of them as the guy who took a shot at me, took out the side window, and hit the headrest in my car. I'm sending you a bill, asshole.

When I got close enough to the detectors, I took off my belt, jacket, and watch, and pulled the keys out of my pocket, dropping everything into a plastic bin to be slid through the machine.

I stepped through the metal detector without setting off any alarms and went to reclaim my articles. Home free - or so I thought.

I had just cinched up my belt when I heard a familiar voice say, "Hey, I know you."

THIRTY

I didn't turn toward the sound, but recognized the voice immediately: It was my old friend from God's Way Church, Beverly.

What the hell is she doing here?

I continued to ignore her as I finished with my belt and began stepping away toward the main auditorium. I hoped that she would think she was mistaken and let it - and me - go. No luck, she intercepted me.

Crap! After all this, she's going to blow my cover!

"I know you," she repeated more stridently as she wobbled toward me.

She was dressed in the same threadbare dark-blue dress I had first seen her in at God's Way Church several weeks prior. Obviously, she hadn't contracted elephantiasis of the feet over the past week or so because her shoes still fit her like the proverbial saddle on a sow.

"I'm sorry, Fraulein," I said, feinting a German accent.

Hearing the accent, she was momentarily put off balance, if that was even possible with her. Her face twisted into an inquisitive snarl and her eyes blinked rapidly.

"I know you," she insisted defiantly, "I never forget a face. You're Ja- "

I caught her by the arm and moved her further away from the security detail. It was difficult the way she wobbled in her high heels and I felt as if I was trying to square dance with someone on stilts.

"Yes, Beverly. I remember now," I said easily, ditching the accent now that I was made.

When we were far enough away, I turned toward her.

"Beverly," I said desperately. "You can't let anybody know that you know me."

"Why?" She blinked. "I - "

"Because I really need you to. It's very important Beverly. Trust me."

"You're with Pathways!" she then accused me angrily. "That's why you're here. I thought you were with the media, but now I know. You were just helping Sommers steal our church!"

Her voice was starting to rise. Even though people were congregating and there was a good din that might mask her voice, I couldn't afford to take the chance that someone might overhear her.

"No I'm not, Beverly," I said angrily under my breath. "I'm not with the media, and I m *not* with Pathways."

Then I turned the tables on her.

"As a matter of fact," I said, "What exactly are *you* doing here?"

She cast her eyes downward and swallowed.

"It…it just seems like that there is no turning back and that God's Way is going to get taken over by Pathways. At least that's what I keep hearing around the church. And I guess I thought I would just check it out for now. That's all."

Then she looked up at me hopefully. She needed approval.

"You believe me, don't you Jack?" she asked.

"Of course I believe you," I said soothingly. "And I don't fault you for coming here. But you know what I don't believe Beverly?"

"What?"

"I don't believe God's Way will get taken over by Pathways."

"You don't? Why?"

"Because I'm going to stop them Beverly. Today, right here, on their own turf."

"How?" she asked. "How can you save us? I've been hearing - "

"I can't tell you," I said, cutting her off. "You'll see in just a little while. But I need your cooperation, Beverly, if I'm going to be successful. Now, can you keep a secret?"

She looked up at me and her eyes blinked rapidly. If I still remembered my Morse code from Boy Scouts, I think she signaled, *Y-E-S*.

"Yes," she promised. "I'm the best at keeping a secret."

"I know you are, Beverly," I said.

Then her voice took on a more desperate tone. "Can you really save us?"

"Yes," I said. "I really can, and I will. You'll see."

She leaned up and kissed me on the cheek.

"Thank-you," she said, and then made a gesture I had read about in Dickens, but had never seen; she touched her index finger to the side of her nose.

"Mum's the word," she said.

"Mum's the word," I repeated.

I smiled and started toward the main auditorium. She trailed along at my side.

"You can't sit with me," I said quietly, staring straight ahead.

"Got it," she acknowledged, in a conspiratorial whisper.

* * *

Due to the fact that people were delayed in getting to their seats because of the security measures, the band didn't strike up right on the dot at ten o'clock and instead allowed a short grace period.

At about ten-fifteen, the lead guitarist, who was also the bandleader, must have gotten a signal because he turned to the rest of the musicians. After a short count they launched into their first number, *Walk by Faith*. Tiffany's voice sounded absolutely dreamy, and I could tell that she was really in her element as an entertainer.

The band played through the customary two songs and the crowd responded with typical enthusiasm, some by standing and swaying to the music with their arms outstretched. Already, the inconveniences of the security checks were long forgotten.

As soon as the number finished, Sommers himself appeared exactly on cue. The band members gently laid down their instruments and walked softly off the stage. When Tiffany disappeared around a corner of the stage, I tried to will her out of harm's way with my mind.

"Get out now Tiffany!" my voice was screaming inside my head. *"Before the shit hits the fan!"*

Sommers was received by the capacity crowd with characteristic enthusiastic applause, and he let it go on for just a short while before holding his hands up to stifle it. When it eased down to just a gentle murmur, he launched into his oratory.

"My good brothers and sisters," he began. "A lot has happened over the past week, and over the past several days. And before we begin praising our Lord, I think it best to remember the word of Ecclesiastes 4:9 '*Two are better than one, because they have a good reward for their toil.*'"

The scripture appeared on the overhead monitors and I saw several people in the crowd nodding in agreement. Some mumbled their approval.

Sommers went on, "And of the Galatians 6:9 '*And let us not grow weary of doing good, for in due season we will reap, if we do not give up.*'"

Again, there were more expressions of approval. Sommers really knew how to lay it on thickly when he needed to.

"And now, my brothers and sisters in Christ, let me set the record straight regarding several important issues."

This had been the moment many people had been waiting for, and I caught a barely perceptible leaning in by the crowd. Sommers might as well have said, "May I have the envelope please?"

"First of all, with respect to the unpleasantness of the security screenings this morning, this was in light of a possible threat to Pathways that our own very capable internal team had detected."

There were some audible gasps in the crowd, and I heard some nervous chatter erupt from pockets of people here and there.

"I know it's hard to imagine that anyone would want to do harm to us, but unfortunately, we have many enemies in our growing secular world: apostates, pagan followers of false religions and prophets, and even and especially, the liberal media with its corrupt government puppets."

Groans and expressions of anger boiled up from the crowd.

"And I assure you that we have taken every precaution to ensure the safety of our flock, and that you are in no danger. This was merely a precaution, and as soon as this threat has passed, we will resume our own, open door policy for The Lord's house."

Sommers brought his arms up from his side and held them out expansively. Several in the crowd rose to their feet, and began aping his gesture.

When they sat down after a few moments, he continued with an update on the status of Pathways.

"As many of you may be aware, the other night we experienced a power failure here at Pathways. I have been assured that this was not an act of terrorism. I repeat, it was *not* an act of terrorism, and this event had nothing to do with our security precautions here today. It was unfortunately, although some may say - not surprisingly, the result of a failure of our government once again to maintain our country's critical infrastructure."

Jeers and boos against our evil and incompetent government could be heard all around. As usual, Sommers was doing a great job of bolstering his *us versus them* battle cry.

"And now, the news that many of you may have heard by the watercooler, but that I want to clarify, to eliminate any confusion, and to stifle any rumors."

Here it comes, I thought.

My beautiful wife, Belinda, has been called away to handle a very important state of affairs at our mission in Sudan. I assure you that everything is fine, and that her talents were needed to deal with a very minor, short-term situation there. She is well and is still travelling across the continent as we speak. I ask you to please keep her in your prayers for a safe journey there, and back home to us."

Several people in the crowd nodded that they would indeed say extra prayers for Belinda's safe return. Then, Sommers dropped a turd into the punchbowl.

"I would also like to announce at this time," Sommers said. "That unfortunately, we will not be having our regular broadcast from our brothers at our missions overseas."

At the mention of this, groans of disappointment rose up from the crowd.

I grinned inwardly and reached down to push the start key on my phone.

Whether the charismatic pastor realized it or not, it was *showtime!*

THIRTY-ONE

"This, I promise you, is due strictly to technical reasons that - " Sommers began to say before all of the overhead monitors suddenly changed to a video of Pathways' overseas missionary, Brother Bob.

The video clip was from a "broadcast" that had yet to be seen by the congregates. I had located it on Bennett's hard drive under the file name: *Brother Bob 17, raw*.

Besides not having seen the video before, the stunned followers of Pathways were also treated to a sight they had not previously been privy to in the other "live stream" events. Now they got to see what Brother Bob was really standing in the front of. And it wasn't a partially completed construction site in the Southern Sudan - he was standing in front of a green screen.

"I...I don't know..." Sommers stammered, and then made some quick motions to the men at the control board to kill the video. The two technicians were befuddled and began checking their monitors and pressing buttons frantically. It was useless. I, or rather Tiffany, had already hacked into the computer-controlled AV console. Zahid had created a special program for me on a flash drive and Tiffany, while flirting with one of the technicians during rehearsal one day, got him to leave his console to get her a glass of water. While he was gone, she installed the malware-containing device. The USB port was on the backside of the unit's CPU, where I knew it wouldn't be detected. Now, it would never be found in time to save Sommers' skin.

"Yes, yes, I'm here Pastor Sommers," Brother Bob recited from his script.

"This…this…" Sommers mumbled.

There was the normal pause in the dialogue, and then Brother Bob said, "Yes, thank-you Pastor Sommers, and hello to you Belinda."

"This, this is a trick!" Sommers suddenly blurted out.

"And as you can see behind me," Brother Bob continued, gesturing to what was nothing more than a green screen like those used by TV weathermen. "We had good day of construction with the school."

"Stop it!" Sommers screamed at the technicians.

The congregates in the crowded auditorium began looking around confused, and talking to one another. Their volume began to rise and they began to stir about anxiously.

"You're right Belinda, I hadn't noticed that," Brother Bob laughed casually down from the monitors.

Sommers was frantic now and sweating profusely. Normally unflappable, his confident demeanor was rapidly vaporizing.

"Turn it off!" he screamed at the technicians. "Turn it off!"

One of the technicians made a hopeless gesture at him. They were trying everything they could, and it was fruitless.

Finally, I felt that the crowd's ire had reached a critical mass. I stood up from my seat.

"They can't turn it off Sommers," I announced to the pastor and to his now tenuous flock. "And you can't stop this now. You are a phony and a cheat. There are no missions overseas. You were just producing videos, and then putting in the backgrounds to make it look like all of these people were doing some good in the world and getting something for their money. In reality though, all you were doing was lining your pockets and buying expensive toys."

"...to answer your question, Pastor Sommers," Brother Bob continued unabated. "Yes, we are already beginning to hold some classes..."

"You're a liar and a sneak!" a familiar voice cried out from the crowd. I turned to see Beverly, up on her feet and wagging an accusatory finger at Sommers.

"No...no, I'm not," Sommers pleaded. Then he pointed back at me. "He... he's the cheat!"

Sommers shifted his attention to a couple of security personnel who were standing at the back of the huge auditorium.

"Arrest this man!" he ordered.

The two men began walking down the aisle to arrest me. Anticipating this, I had purposely sat in the middle of the row. If they wanted to get to me to manhandle me out of there, they would have to get past several of Pathways' members, many of whom were becoming visibly angry with what they were watching unfold.

"...right Belinda. I agree," Brother Bob replied to no one.

"And you're trying to steal the God's Way Church!" Beverly went on. "That's what you're trying to do!"

The goons were at the end of the aisle, trying to get people to move out of the way so they could get to me. The group remained defiant and wouldn't budge. One man, about three seats from the end, stood up and yelled out, "I'm not moving an inch until I find out exactly what's going on here! I've given a lot of money to this church over the years, and I'm not leaving until I know where it's been going!"

Others chimed in with their approvals.

"I...I assure you - " Sommers pleaded desperately, only to be interrupted by Brother Bob on the screen.

"...fixed our problems with local suppliers, Pastor Sommers..."

Sommers turned to the giant screen, "Shut up!" he screamed.

"You want him to stop talking to you and Belinda Sommers?" I asked. "Great. Brother Bob's going to talk to the congregation right now."

I turned and looked about to the crowd.

"Do you good people want to see how your money is *really* being spent?" I asked them.

A chorus of "yeahs" rose up around me.

"Watch," I said, and pushed a key on my phone.

The screen changed to another video of Brother Bob. He was staring into the camera and this time, the background of the fantasy construction site in Sudan had returned.

"Hello," he began. "I'm Brother Bob broadcasting from the Pathways' mission in Southern Sudan."

He clicked his finger and the background image disappeared.

"Except, I'm not really in the Southern Sudan."

As he said this, he began peeling off his blond beard and mustache to reveal a clean-shaven face underneath. "And my name is not Bob," he announced.

The crowd around me gasped, even the security team was transfixed.

The man then pulled off a blond wig and tossed it off to the side.

"My name is Matthew Gregory, and I'm an actor."

One of the other gems I had gleaned from Bennett's hard drive, were several of the scripts for these charades, as well as the actual names of the actors they were assigned to. A quick search on IMDb for Matthew Gregory had revealed what I had suspected when I first discovered the phony video files; he was a struggling actor who did bit parts in low-budget films and probably took part in this subterfuge to help pay his rent. After I lured him into meeting me by purporting to be a big time producer, I confronted him with the tapes and told him to play ball, or as they say, "you'll never work in this town again."

Seeing how they had been conned, the crowd sat silently stunned. I looked up to the stage at Sommers. He was hunched over like an inflatable doll whose air was escaping.

"…and I was paid by Pathways Church to do a series of videos at a small studio in Riverside, California. I never knew what the videos were for, and I needed the money. But now I know what they were being used for and I'm sorry for being a part of this deception to cheat you out of your money. I'm sorry, and I hope you'll find it in your Christian hearts to forgive me."

"I want my money back!" a man screamed from the crowd.

"Me too!" another chimed in.

"Keep your grubby hands off of God's Way Church!" Beverly bellowed, her fist pounding at the air.

Just then, Bennett appeared from offstage. He ran out to within a few feet of Sommers and pointed an angry finger at me.

"Get that bastard!" he screamed at the security personnel.

At this command from Bennett, more members of the audience around me stood up in defiance, blocking the security guards. The guards looked helplessly toward Bennett.

Then Bennett drew out his gun.

THIRTY-TWO

"Get him!" Bennett screamed again, pointing the gun in my direction,

At the sight of the gun, people began screaming and clamoring to get out of their seats. The auditorium erupted into a scene of pandemonium.

Sommers gazed around at his crumbling empire in disbelief. Then he looked at Bennett.

"No," he pleaded desperately. "You can't do this."

Bennett looked quickly at the scrambling crowd and then at Sommers. Then he turned the gun on the Pathways' pastor and shot him in the chest.

The sound of the gunshot echoed through the giant hall and sent the crowd into an even more frenzied response. People had taken to climbing over the tops of the chairs now to get out, some trampling others in their way. It was a scene of bedlam. The Lord's house had become a madhouse!

Bennett dashed off the stage and left Sommers lying on his back, bleeding out.

I climbed over the empty seatback in front of me and began stepping over the seats one by one. It was slow going and I had to straddle them gingerly, but it was no use trying to battle the crush of people in the aisles, especially since I would be swimming against the tide. I turned quickly and noted that the security personnel weren't trying to follow me; they had either given up themselves, or were trampled by the mob.

I reached Sommers and could see as I moved closer to him that he was still breathing. But it wouldn't be for long; the bullet had hit him in the left lung, and already I could hear the gurgling sound of a sucking chest wound. He wasn't going to make it anyway, so I went for broke and grabbed him by the jacket collar to get his attention.

"Belinda!" I screamed. "Or Sara! Where the hell is she?"

He sputtered and blood dribbled out of his mouth.

"Where is she!" I repeated.

"Basement," he managed to choke out. "In the basement."

I shook my head, trying to recall the plans to the church that Tiffany had drawn out. I didn't know about a basement. Maybe it was off-site somewhere at a safe house.

"Where?" I yelled. "Basement where?"

"Bennett's office," Sommers wheezed. A bubble of bloody saliva came out of the corner of his mouth. "Behind the bookcase. Secret door…"

He coughed and then gagged as his mouth filled with blood. Then his body convulsed a few times, and he was gone, his lifeless eyes staring up to the giant monitor above the stage.

I debated whether or not to go back and get my gun, but then I saw the crowd was jamming up the exits. There was no way I could get to the bathroom in time.

I ran off the stage, into the main hallway, and into Bennett's office.

There was no receptionist in the outer office, and the door to Bennett's was left open. I ran in and saw that one of his bookcases had been moved to the side, exposing an open doorway. I ran to the doorway and down the short flight of stairs that led to a small room underneath.

The room was only about the size of a small bathroom, and had only a commode, a sink, and a single bed in it. The bed had leather restraints attached to the frame. The restraints were open and the bed was empty.

I stared at it for a moment, recalling my visit to Pathways that other night and the sounds I had heard while in Bennett's office.

Was that Sara? Had she been right below me?

Just then I heard another sound, a thumping sound, rhythmic. It was the beat of a helicopter's main rotor blades; Bennett was escaping from the roof.

Crap!

I raced out of Bennett's office, into the main hallway, and through the door that lead to the stairway to the roof. I sprinted up the stairs, two at a time, and opened the door to the roof just in time to see the big twin turbine powered Augusta A109 as it approached for touchdown on the helipad.

Bennett was standing off to the edge and was holding Sara at his side. His hand gripped her wrist roughly and he had his gun out. They both turned away from the rotor wash as it kicked up dirt and the tiny aggregate material from the roof. When they turned away, Bennett saw me and drew his gun up.

He fired just as I dodged back into the stairwell.

Zing!

A bullet ricocheted off the concrete blocks.

When I heard the turbine speed decrease, I knew that they were boarding the helicopter, and figured it might be my only chance.

I poked my head back out and saw Bennett shoving Sara into the back cabin of the helicopter. He didn't climb in after her, and instead got into the left, co-pilot seat in the front of the aircraft. I remembered then from my research that Pathways' operations chief was training to be a pilot.

Hell of a time to take a lesson, I thought.

I dashed out from my cover to the right side of the helicopter, opposite of Bennett, and grabbed a handful of the tiny white stones that served as aggregate for the roof.

I jumped up onto the fairing that covered the helicopter's landing gear and dumped the rocks into the intake screen for one of the helicopter's turbine engines. The rocks were smaller than the screen opening and they got sucked down into the rapidly spinning blades.

There was a terrible screeching sound followed by a loud thump as the rocks hit the blades and destroyed several of them in what is known in aviation parlance as FOD or "foreign object damage."

The aircraft had twin engines, but it may not have been able to lift off with only one.

I heard more screeching then as additional blades disintegrated, and blew out the exhaust opening. With one engine destroying itself, the aircraft was beginning to lose power. I looked over to the pilot and he was frantically checking his instruments and handling alarms in the cockpit.

This was my opportunity.

I opened the right hand side main cabin door to where Sara was sitting. Thankfully, Bennett hadn't bothered to put her seat belt on, and I reached in and dragged her out onto the roof. She looked at me oddly, like she didn't recognize me. Then I remembered that she wouldn't.

"It's me, Jack!" I screamed above the rotor wash and the roar of the engines. "Get out of here!"

I shoved her toward the corner of the building, and she lowered her head and ran for the stairwell.

Boom!

Through the helicopter's open doorway, Bennett had fired another shot at me. Thankfully, he missed. I ducked off to the side of the copter, but I could still see into the cockpit.

The pilot was animated and gesturing to his instruments angrily; he didn't want to try to lift off with a damaged engine. Bennett yelled something back at him, and then put the gun to the pilot's head.

"Hey Bennett!" I yelled.

Hearing my voice, Bennett was momentarily distracted and turned away long enough for the pilot to open his door and bail out; he obviously wasn't getting paid enough for a suicide mission like this.

The pilot ran across the roof toward the open doorway of the stairwell to where Sara was still waiting for me.

Damn it, I wish she would just go.

I turned my attention back to Bennett and saw him look from me, to the pilot, to the controls. He reached down with his hand and grabbed the control stick. I saw him push the overhead throttle levers, and the RPM of the left side engine increased. The right side was still limping along. Could he lift off with the available power?

I stepped down and grabbed another handful of rocks and slung them into the intake of the right side engine. It screeched and shuddered again as more blades were destroyed. Fire came out of the engine exhaust and the aircraft began shuddering violently from the imbalance of the turbine blades.

I felt the craft begin to bounce and then lift off, and I stepped off the fairing and onto the roof. All I could do now was to pray that Bennett couldn't get very far with only one engine, and that the authorities could apprehend him in short order. I ran to the open stairway door and to where Sara was huddled.

"Where's the pilot?" I yelled to her.

She pointed down the stairway. "He just ran right past me," she said.

Coward, I thought, and turned my attention back to the Augusta as it tried to lift off.

Sara and I heard the whine as Bennett pushed both throttle controls to their stops. The aircraft began to lift off, and he feathered the tail rotor to spin the aircraft to the north. With a loud whump-whumping of the blades, the Augusta pitched forward and began to climb higher off from the roof.

Damn it; the bastard was going to get away.

Then…

BOOM!

The right side engine completely disintegrated. A huge cloud of black smoke belched out of the exhaust opening. The copter spun around wildly then tilted sideways. Bennett fought furiously with the controls to manage the engine loss, but it was no match for his limited experience. The Augusta pitched nose down, and the main rotor blades hit the edge of the walls of the atrium and shattered, pieces whizzing off the roof. With no lift and pointing nose down, the body of the craft disappeared from our sight and fell like a rock, three stories down into the atrium of the Pathways Church. It exploded in a huge fireball, as over two-hundred gallons of fuel was ignited by the hot engines. Burning shrapnel began to rain down on the roof.

Sara turned to try to run down the stairway, but I grabbed her by the arm.

"Not that way," I said. "The building could be fully engulfed before long and we won't get out. I know another way."

"Over here," I said, and pointed to the roof ladder I had used just the other morning.

We sprinted past the pieces of burning aircraft and got to the edge.

"You go first," I said to Sara. "But take it slow. You're safe from the fire and explosions as soon as you get over the edge."

She hoisted her leg over the low roof wall and grabbed onto the ladder rails. She went down slowly with my encouragement, and before long, was on the ground. Then I climbed over myself just as the heat from the fuel-fed inferno was beginning to scorch my face.

* * *

On the ground I grabbed Sara and we ran to my car in the parking structure.

Not surprisingly, it was chaotic. Between the shooting and now the explosion, all of the congregates were desperately trying to get out, and emergency personnel were trying just as desperately to get in. Sirens screamed and car horns honked incessantly, creating a deafening din inside the concrete structure.

I didn't care about all of the confusion and got Sara to my trusty minivan. I clicked the key fob, opened the back door, and shoved her into the rear seat.

"Get down on the floor and stay down," I said to her. "If you want me to help you disappear, no one can see you from this point on. Got it?"

She nodded mutely, and then got down on the floor.

I ran around to the driver's side and was just pulling on the handle when I heard a voice behind me.

"Hey there."

I turned and it was Beverly, she was smiling and she hobbled toward me.

"You really did do it, didn't you?" she said. "You exposed Pathways for who they really were, and you probably saved God's Way in the process."

I paused for a moment and took a deep breath, reflecting on what she had said. She was right; I probably did save God's Way.

"Yes," I said finally. "I think I did."

She looked up at me and smiled her goofy smile.

"Thank-you," she said, "Thank-you - whatever your name really is."

I looked back down at her.

"It's Jack, Beverly," I said. "One Eyed Jack."
Then I kissed her.
…And she didn't even blink.

EPILOGUE

By the time the fire department arrived on the scene to battle the blaze at Pathways Church, the building was fully engulfed and it took several battalions to knock it down. Miraculously, there were no fatalities from the fire, although several injuries were reported. Otherwise though, the structure and its contents were considered a total loss.

The ensuing investigation by police and the FBI as to what had happened that fateful Sunday was stymied by the fact that the DVR for the extensive security system cameras had been completely destroyed in the inferno. The absence of this vital investigative tool meant that the officials had to try to rely on the eyewitness accounts - all four thousand of them - to try to sort things out. Good luck with that.

The charred remains of Sommers' and Bennett's bodies were recovered from the fire, and DNA tests positively identified then as Robert William Kennings of Cincinnati, Ohio and Stephan Bellamy of Milton, Florida respectively.

Kennings had a colorful rap sheet, and had worked variously as a scam artist, a pimp, and a gigolo. And Bellamy was the notorious Reverend Bellamy, a former evangelist of the defunct Souls United Church. He had skipped town and been on the lam for several years after bilking thousands of followers out of untold amounts of money. He had also been convicted in absentia of tax fraud.

Several offshore accounts with undisclosed amounts of money had been traced back to Bellamy, and the investigation was ongoing.

The biggest mystery that the authorities struggled to unravel was the strange disappearance of Belinda Sommers. Agents assigned to the case had raided the Sommers' home and through DNA samples found at the scene, determined that she was in fact the fugitive Sara Kelly, who had escaped from prison several years prior and had not been seen since. With this latest twist, officials reinstated her status on the FBI's ten most wanted list, and vowed to capture her and bring her to justice once and for all.

After having her appearance altered, I moved Sara to a safe house I had the use of, deep in the hills of Topanga Canyon outside of Los Angeles. Hearing the news that she had now catapulted herself back into the FBI's spotlight, she discussed with me the sobering possibility of turning herself in and, as she said, "just getting it over with."

I believe in justice, but I also believed her story that she had been innocent with regards to the murder in which she was charged as an accessory. I convinced her that at this juncture in her life, if she turned herself in, she would be spending the rest of her days in jail. "Wouldn't it be better to repay society by doing something positive with your life, as opposed to rotting away in a cell?" I countered.

She agreed that would be a better outcome, and I began to call in a bunch of favors. Within a couple of weeks, she had a new name, a new passport, and was on her way to Columbia, South America. I had connected her with a church group that I knew of, and she was going to help them run a shelter for homeless women and their children. The facility taught the mothers new life skills, and helped them and their children to get back on their feet. She had slipped into the shadows and was safe from extradition as long as she kept her nose clean, which she promised to do.

I forbade her to ever contact me, but she apparently defied me because I got an anonymous e-mail a month or so later that read:

After all my time faking it, I am finally feeling blessed to do The Lord's work. I can't thank-you enough for believing in me, and for saving me. I have accepted God in my heart, and he is leading me on the correct path in my life. May God bless you.

In his service.

With regards to other church business, second in command, Pastor Jim Harkin agreed to take the reins and act as interim pastor of God's Way Church until a permanent one could be chosen. Harkin had very eloquently stated in a message on the church's website that it was time for some new blood to carry the torch forward. Betty Mentzer had very bravely stepped up to be the new head of the women's ministry, and she was to be capably assisted by none other than my old friend and partner in crime, Beverly.

On the home front, after postponing the kickoff of her tour for a couple of weeks, Tiffany finally hit the road and was now playing to sold out houses from coast to coast. Her manager stated unequivocally that it was one of the most successful tours he had ever booked, and that he expected big things to come from it. For her part, Tiffany was enjoying the excitement of the road, and was reveling in the realization that she was finally able to live the dream she had abandoned so long ago.

After making sure that I wouldn't get in the way, I had decided to take a break from things and was travelling on the tour with her. It was great to be able to hear her perform every night, and to watch her bring down the house with a fan base that was growing exponentially with every new show.

During the downtime, I'd still check e-mails, and try to keep tabs on business back in LA. I was limited in what I could accomplish, and I knew that doing it remotely wasn't the same as being on my home turf. But I wasn't really worried about it. If one of my marks skipped a payment, or if some juicy new case slipped through my nets, it was really no big deal to me. Because after all, my name is One Eyed Jack, and I know that there will always be people with secrets to hide.

The End

If you have enjoyed this book, you have made me very happy, and have validated my work as a writer. A review on Amazon or Goodreads would be most appreciated. If you would like to read some of my other works, they are listed below:

SHORT STORIES (Available as e-books at Amazon.com)

The Loot

The Last Seduction

Promise of the Future

One Eyed Jack (short story)

BOOKS: Non-Fiction (Available as print or e-book at Amazon.com)

Eddie: The life and times of America's preeminent bad boy

BOOKS: Fiction (Available as print or e-book at Amazon.com)

One Eyed Jack

Russian Roulette (the second in the One Eyed Jack series)

One Eyed Jack video trailer: www.youtube.com/watch?v=XvraVL8dMY0

My website: www.christopherjlynch.com

Jack is back!

Blue Chip - *the fourth book in the One Eyed Jack series*

An extortion attempt on a steroid smuggler leads Jack into the fast-paced world of college football and high-stakes sports betting. Before long, America's favorite blackmailer finds himself trying to save the reputation - and the life - of a promising college football star who is being blackmailed into becoming a human guinea pig for the mob.

Available in 2016

About the Author

Los Angeles native Christopher J. Lynch has written for numerous local and national publications, as well as the authorized biography of the iconic child actor Ken Osmond, (Eddie Haskell from the TV series *Leave it To Beaver*).

A lover of crime fiction, he has published several short stories, and is the author of the *One Eyed Jack* series about a professional blackmailer who operates in and around the South Bay area of Los Angeles. The debut novel in the series was a 2013 Shamus Award finalist, and a 2014 Writers Digest honorable mention for genre fiction. Christopher has recently optioned the movie rights to One Eyed Jack to a major Hollywood studio who plans to adapt it into a feature film.

All of Christopher's work is self-published, and he likes to give back to the writing community by offering free self-publishing seminars at libraries and other organizations.

When he's not writing, Christopher enjoys mountain climbing, and has reached the summits of Mount Whitney, Mount Kilimanjaro in Africa, and most recently, completed a trek to Mount Everest Base Camp in Nepal. He once trained and led eleven blind hikers to the summit of 10,000 foot Mount Baldy, the highest point in Los Angeles County, and the third highest point in Southern California. A documentary film is being made of the adventure. You can view a trailer of the film at: www.baldyfortheblind.com

Christopher's website is www.christopherjlynch.com

Made in the USA
San Bernardino, CA
13 November 2015